IRONMAN

Also by Chris Crutcher

IRONMAN

a novel by
CHRIS CRUTCHER

Greenwillow Books

N E W Y O R K

Copyright © 1995 by Chris Crutcher
All rights reserved. No part of this book
may be reproduced or utilized in any form
or by any means, electronic or mechanical,
including photocopying, recording, or by
any information storage and retrieval
system, without permission in writing
from the Publisher, Greenwillow Books,
a division of William Morrow & Company, Inc.,
1350 Avenue of the Americas, New York, NY 10019.

Printed in the United States of America
First Edition 10 9 8 7 6 5 4 3 2

Library of Congress Cataloging-in-Publication Data
Crutcher, Chris.
Ironman / by Chris Crutcher.
      p.   cm.
    Summary: While training for a triathlon, seventeen-
year-old Bo attends an anger management group at school
which leads him to examine his relationship with his father.
ISBN 0-688-13503-X
[1. Interpersonal relations—Fiction.
2. Fathers and sons—Fiction.
3. Triathlon—Fiction.]   I. Title.
PZ7.C89Ir   1995
[Fic]—dc20
94-1657   CIP   AC

In memory of my mom—
1922–1994

CHAPTER 1

> TO: *Larry King*
>
> RE: *Exclusive rights to an hour-long interview immediately prior to publication of the soon-to-be highly-sought-after memoirs of our country's future premier Ironman, Beauregard Brewster, in the year of his quest to conquer the field in Yukon Jack's Eastern Washington Invitational Scabland Triathlon.*

OCTOBER 10

Dear Larry,

At 4:30 each morning I awaken to your voice. I lie transfixed until five—when I haul my aching body out of the sack for another in a series of infinite workouts—listening to the wise men and loons of yesterday's airways deliver opinions on everything from the hole in the ozone layer (it covers an area larger than the United States) to antidepressants (Dick Cavett and Patty Duke swear by them; Scientologists swear at them) to racism (you smell out racial prejudice like my father smells out Democrats) to the most effective methods to forever rid oneself of fat globules and cellulite (there aren't any) to the whereabouts of Elvis (Jeffrey Dahmer ate him). What I like about you is, you listen. You interview politicians and movie stars and musicians and every kind of hero and villain. And authors. When you are finally accorded the privilege of reaching across the mike to shake my sweaty hand, I'll be one of those. It's gonna be a career-making interview, Larry, and to give you full opportunity for the preparation it deserves, I've decided to leak the memoirs to you as they happen.

I am aware from your numerous comments that you have not long been such a prudent caretaker of your physical self (your heart attack set you in the right direction) and may not know that a triathlete (AKA Ironman) is a swimming, bicycling, running lunatic, willing and able to cover great distances at high speeds while enduring extreme physical pain. That's me, Lar, and you shall be privy to the circumstances surrounding my voyage beyond human physical limits in my crusade to finish Yukon Jack's E. W. Invitational Scabland extravaganza alive, and well ahead of all competitors under voting age. You should know that Yukon Jack's is not your run of the mill, rapid-stroll-through-hell event. Distances in a normal, Olympic-length triathlon are such that participants spend approximately twice as much time cycling as they do running or swimming, giving a definite edge to the good bikers. But Yukon Jack, AKA Jack McCoy, is a two-time English Channel swimmer and a three-time finisher of the Western States 100-mile ultra-marathon, and he's the first person to tell you he thinks most cyclists are more interested in displaying their tight, multicolored costumes than they are in "gettin' down to some real physical exercise," so he shaved their edge off this particular event by doubling the swimming distance and halving the biking distance. All that works to my advantage because I love to train swimming and running, but whenever I ride a bike more than three blocks, I feel the need for major surgery to remove that skinny little seat.

Unfortunately, to reach the physical, spiritual, and emotional heights required to conquer this event, I must also endure my regular life and the mortals who would stand in my way. One of those mortals, not the greatest nor the least, would be Keith Redmond, my English teacher and the head football coach at Clark Fork High School. Redmond has not forgiven my cardinal sin of walking out on the football team on the second day of two-a-days this year because I took issue—quite vocally, I have to admit—with his practice of public humiliation as a motivator. I'm a bit on the skinny side, though I like to call it wiry, so you wouldn't think by looking at me that any football coach would spend more than fifteen seconds grieving my departure, but I've got some sticky fingers when it comes to hauling in the old pigskin, and Redmond was expecting league-leading numbers out of me this season. So when I took my eyes off a ball I should have caught, because I was burrowing into the grass to avoid crippling whiplash at the hands of Kyle Gifford— who mounts on his bedroom wall pictures of *teammates* whose seasons he has ended—Redmond stormed into my face, battering at my chest as if his index finger were a woodpecker, and demanded at maximum decibels for me to declare my gender. It was our third confrontation of the day, so I told him I was a sissy and he was an asshole, and I threw down my helmet and headed for the showers.

Looking back it was probably an overreaction, but I don't do well with degradation, and that isn't likely to change. I could have saved myself a lot of grief if I'd transferred out of Coach's Senior English class because he makes no secret about what he thinks of quitters, but I thought I owed it to him to hang around and torment him a little. It was a bad idea.

This morning Mr. Serbousek stepped into the hall between second and third periods, motioning me into his classroom. He said, "Congratulations, Brewster, you're over the top. You have my unofficial county record."

Damn. "Redmond got me suspended." It was not a question.

"Looks that way."

"How long?"

Mr. S said, "Indefinitely."

"That's a long time."

"You want the exit speech?"

"About holding my temper?"

He nodded.

"About accountability? About being seventeen years old and an infinitesimal quarter-step from adulthood?" I squinted, indicating an infinitesimal quarter-step between my thumb and forefinger. "About being held responsible for my own actions? Managing my impulses?"

Mr. S smiled. "If anyone asks, tell them *I* said those things."

"Affirmative, sir. You certainly have your work cut out for you."

"Meaning?"

"I've got you beat for *number* of suspensions in the county within recorded history, but you're still ahead on total days. If I'm out more than nine, I'm the undisputed county champ. You'd lose esteem."

"Records were made to be broken," he said. "I'm mature now, my challenges lie in different arenas. That one stood more than eight years, a record in itself. Don't count on me this time, buddy. My act is wearing thin around here as far as you're concerned. Be prepared to kiss some unsavory butts to get out of this one."

I said, "The law says they owe me an education."

"But it doesn't say what kind. That education could consist of home tutoring two hours a day with Mrs. Conroy."

A sobering thought for me, Larry. Conroy's been voted Female Teacher Most Likely to Take a Life three years running. The woman can't teach a lick; they'd be killing two birds with one stone. Better polish my pucker.

"Bo," Mr. Serbousek said as I reached the door.

"Yeah?"

"Did you really use the A-word again?"

I was unrepentant, Mr. King. "Yes sir, I did."

4

He shook his head slowly. "Why?"

"Short and to the point, sir, like you teach us in Journalism. You know, 'Why use a rambling phrase when a simple one-word description will do?' As true for spoken language as it is for the written word."

At my locker, I stuffed my backpack with enough textbooks to keep me busy "indefinitely" and headed for the bike rack to collect my mountain bike. I probably should have just split, but I couldn't resist circling the main building three times, no hands, turning sideways on the seat and spreading my arms wide—crucifixion-style—as I passed the windows of Redmond's classroom. Then I coasted out onto the neighborhood street and headed toward the two-lane.

My ouster came at an opportune time, actually. I was due at work at my janitorial job at the Clark Fork Free Press by six and had been juggling time like crazy to squeeze in a workout. So I reset the chronograph on my watch, snapped the plastic clasp of my backpack tight around my waist, and leaned onto the handlebars, knowing I could ride hard for a good hour and a half, stop up at the university weight room for an hour, and still take a leisurely whirlpool before picking up my little brother at the day care and depositing him at home. Life was good, Larry.

When Mom and Dad find out about the suspension, life will become bad.

I focused my thoughts on this morning's confrontation with Redmond and pedaled hard into the long incline just past the city limits on the south side of town. Clark Fork, a town of less than ten thousand if you don't count the university population, sits near the southwest border of Spokane County, about seventeen miles outside the "big city." If not for Clark Fork University, it would probably be just another conservative eastern Washington wheat town believing in the universal sanctity of bearing arms, but the staff of the university carries equal weight with the NRA lobby, and according to *Spokane* magazine it's probably one of the most politically and environmentally well-balanced spots in the state.

Fall here is my favorite time of year. Rolling wheat fields stretch to a golden infinity, and a cool wind pressed against my face as my knobby tires hummed over the smooth blacktop. I won't ride the mountain bike in Yukon Jack's—I have a racer for that—but it's great for training; for one thing, the seat is wider and softer and does not extend three feet into my large intestine.

As the incline steepened, I increased my rhythm, welcoming the burning in my thighs. I'm able to endure these monster workouts because I welcome physical pain when struggles at school or home heat up. I understand physical pain; I can control it.

Sometimes I think the Redmonds of the world were put here for no reason other than to test me. I mean, I never see that guy coming. Here he is this morning, fingering through the stack of Senior Comp papers *most* of us just turned in. He gazes at us over his reading glasses. "Miss Clairborne," he says, "your paper seems to be missing."

"I gave it to you yesterday, remember?" Annie Clairborne says. "I didn't know if I'd be here today, and I wanted to be sure you didn't mark it late."

"Indeed you did, young lady," Redmond says back, like some kindly grandpa with a short-term memory deficit. "Indeed you did. My apologies." He stacks the papers neatly on the corner of the desk and stands. Redmond is one immense dude, all of six feet four and about two-thirty-five, with muscles stacked on his arms like an ancient pile of cannonballs. The material of his suit coat stretches tight as a trampoline across the back of those massive shoulders, and his thighs constantly threaten to split the legs of his slacks.

So he sits on the edge of his desk, Larry, running those thick fingers over his balding dome, adjusting his tie, and I still don't know he's coming after me. Then he gazes above our heads, out the bank of windows at the back of the room. "Mr. Brewster," he says quietly, and I finally hear the whistle of the oncoming train.

"Yes sir?"

"Apart from Miss Clairborne, you appear to be the only class member who failed to deposit a paper on my desk this morning. *You* didn't give me a paper yesterday that I've also forgotten, did you, Mr. Brewster? I mean, I'm not losing my mind here, am I, son?"

I've speculated aloud on the whereabouts of Redmond's mind in the past, to great consequence. "No sir," I say. "I think your mind is right where it's supposed to be."

He ignores my insolence. "Then where is your assignment?"

I say, "I'm not finished with it. I wasn't here the day it was assigned and—"

"Of course you got the assignment from someone who was here."

"Uh, actually, I sort of spaced it. I—"

"So you don't know exactly what the assignment *was*."

I say, "Not exactly," and Larry, I'm feeling the monster within me stir a bit. "But—"

"So," Redmond says, "your saying 'I'm not finished' is something of a smoke screen, don't you agree? In point of fact, you haven't even begun."

"Well . . ." The monster growls. Enduring public humiliation is not my strong suit.

"Mr. Brewster—your full name is Beauregard, isn't that correct? Do you mind if I call you Beauregard?"

He knows my name is Beauregard, Larry. I played football for him for three years. When this is over, I think, I need to remember this moment as the point of no return. I say, "Actually, only my friends call me that."

"Well, I'm considering myself a friend, even if you don't," Redmond says. "I'm going to be enough of a friend, *Beau-re-gard*, to remind you that if you continue in the direction you're headed, and have been headed for some time—probably since you walked out on the football team—your life will come to little consequence. Is it not true, *Beau-re-gard*, that on the day you missed this assignment, you were in fact skipping school, and that you put your mother in the position of writing us a deceptive note to get you back in?"

Man, how does he find this shit out? "Are you calling my mother a liar?" Weak try, Brewster.

"I'm calling your mother unfortunate," Redmond says right back at me. "Unfortunate because she's placed in the position of having to put her need to have her son *Beau-re-gard* in school over her integrity. By the way, does your mother call you *Beau-re-gard*? Is your mother your friend?"

The monster speaks. "Does your wife call you *asshole*?" were my last words in English class for the day, and probably for some time.

I don't get it. It's October 10 for chrissakes, and this is my third suspension. I'm a nice guy, Larry. I don't do drugs, don't usually cut class—though Redmond was right about my cutting the day he gave the comp assignment—rarely fight, and usually turn in my homework, or at least somebody's homework with my name on it. But when my back is against the wall, my mouth is a machine gun. Don't think it's easy to explain to the principal, or your parents, why you called your English teacher an asshole. I mean, I'm literally clutching at the word to stuff it back down my throat as it sprays between my lips on the one hand, and celebrating a direct hit on the other. I need to remember I'm lobbing road apples and Redmond's lobbing A-bombs.

This is good stuff, Larry, and is to be continued.

Your humble scribe,

Beauregard Brewster

Lionel Serbousek ambles into the principal's office and pours himself a cup of coffee.

Dr. Stevens looks up from a pile of papers, leaning back in her chair. "Ah," she sighs, "the not-so-cowardly Lion. Make yourself right at home."

"Thought you'd feel that way," he says, wincing as the coffee burns his tongue. He gazes around the room. "Brings back old memories."

Dr. Stevens smiles. "It ought to," she says. "You certainly spent enough time in my office back at Frost."

"You were the vice-principal," he says, "and I was the principal of vice. We were made for each other back then."

"So now that you're a teacher, why hasn't that changed?"

"I'm aware that the coffee's much better here than in the teachers' lounge."

"I make more money than teachers do," Dr. Stevens says. "Good coffee is one way I remind myself how far I've come and how far you haven't."

Lion nods. "Sensitive leadership. That's why I followed you to the boonies."

"You followed me to the boonies because I was the only educator in four northwestern states who knew you and still wanted to hire you. I assume you're here because of Bo."

Lion nods. "That kid's a variation on my mother's curse."

"How so?"

"When I was little, before the accident, my mom used to hope I'd live long enough to have kids just like me. I figured I'd outsmarted her with my life-style, but now here's Brewster. He ain't my kid, but he might as well be."

"The universe works in strange and mysterious ways," Dr. Stevens says, smiling, "that we, in our earthly ignorance—"

"—get pickaxed by every time," Lion says.

"The gospel according to Serbousek."

"So what do I have to do to get him back in class?"

"You mean, what does *he* have to do to get back in class."

"Whatever."

Dr. Stevens shakes her head. "I sure wish he'd stop calling Mr. Redmond an asshole."

"When it's a less apt description, maybe he will. I used to ask you this all the time when I was being sent home, but how come teachers never get in trouble? How come it's always the kid who eats it?"

"The kid doesn't have a union."

"Man, if I ran this school—"

"Don't get it into your head that I do," Dr. Stevens says. "I'm the principal here, not the owner. Remember, the same flexibility that allows a Lionel Serbousek allows a Keith Redmond."

"Now *that's* scary."

"No scarier for you than for Keith." Dr. Stevens stands and walks to the coffeepot, and Lionel notices yet again what a stunning woman she is. Tall and very dark, lean in an athletic way—the first black female vice-principal in the Spokane school district before she moved to Clark Fork to take a principal's job she believed would never be offered in the city. Lion would have crawled to the northern slope in his swimming trunks in mid-January to teach in her school, given how she stood behind his fierce sense of justice back at Robert Frost High in Spokane through the mid-eighties.

"So what should I tell Bo?"

"Tell him he needs to contact me. Mr. Redmond and he and I will have a meeting as soon as Bo requests it."

"What's the bottom line?"

Dr. Stevens grimaces. "You're going to love this. Keith says he won't allow Bo back into his class until he's enrolled in Mr. Nakatani's anger management group."

"That's two hours two mornings a week. The kid's in training and he works. That's too much, Gail. Not to mention, that's a pretty rough group."

"It's not that bad," Dr. Stevens says. "Mr. Nak's good, really good. And even though Bo denies an anger problem, he told me himself he fantasizes Keith buried to the neck in a red anthill at high noon in Death Valley in mid-July."

"Hell," Lion says, "that's a healthy fantasy. I have it all the time, except I pour honey on his eyeballs."

"Unfortunately, I can't order you into Mr. Nak's anger management group."

"What if Bo refuses?"

"This is his third time out. I'd have to give him home tutoring."

"Conroy?"

Dr. Stevens smiles. "Conroy."

CHAPTER 2

Dear Larry,

The Clark Fork University athletic complex hummed with college kids changing classes shortly after noon when I dropped my fake student ID card onto the equipment room counter where the student attendant passes out locker keys and racquetball rackets and such. I dug my shorts and a sleeveless sweatshirt out of the small workout bag I carry on the back of my bike, and within minutes was lost among the forest of weight machines and exercise equipment I hope will speed my metamorphosis into a true Ironman. (A *true* Ironman participates in the Hawaiian Ironman contest, where he—or she—swims about two-and-a-half miles, bikes a hundred, and runs a full marathon, but, hey, one step at a time.) Apart from two Schwarzenegger types taking turns spotting each other in the free-weight area and a really sleek, powerful-looking girl doing battle with a rowing machine, who I was afraid to look at for reasons of self-esteem—and lust—the room was empty.

I approached the wall of mirrors behind the free weights for a quick appraisal, locking my knees to flex the thighs, then rocking back on my heels to study the calves. Pretty good muscle definition in the ol' legs if I do say so, Larry, but they still more resemble pipe cleaners than the well-oiled pistons I envision. I pulled up my sweatshirt to reveal my best feature, a truly symmetrical washboard stomach, then jerked the shirt quickly over my head, spun a one-eighty and flexed the lats, hoping for even a hint of that cobra look. A hint is what I saw. This is the body that led Camille Patterson to comment—loudly, at high noon in the student lunchroom—that I could tread water in a garden hose, and I have a feeling it'll be a while before anyone calls me the Wedge. I checked back over my shoulder to be certain the girl on the rowing machine wasn't getting aerobic, laughing at my performance.

I focus my weight workouts on endurance, routinely setting each machine to the maximum weight at which I can squeeze out twelve repetitions, then drop it ten pounds, crank out maximum reps, drop another ten, max reps, until I'm pushing almost no weight and the particular muscle I'm working on has turned to oatmeal. Between each machine I work an automatic StairMaster for five minutes at full speed. The entire workout takes an hour and ten minutes: upper body one day, legs the next. Today I popped a self-recorded, made-for-pain Bob Seger/ Bruce Springsteen/Rod Stewart tape into my Walkman, set the volume to OED (Optimum Eardrum Damage), and focused on Redmond's face with each and every repetition. Each time I believed I couldn't eke out one more, I'd picture that peckerhead parked behind his smirk, accenting all three syllables of my name, and the resulting surge of power brought full extension. I should thank the man; he may single-handedly transform me into the behemoth I long to be.

It's interesting how he zeroed in on me after I quit football, Lar. You'd have thought he'd just forget about my scrawny butt and get on with his season, but he's demanded that players caught talking to me run the hill after practice till they throw up. I'm told it's called a Brewster when anyone lets up before the whistle. I guess fame comes at a price.

When I climbed back onto my mountain bike outside the university weight room to head for my little brother's day care, I could barely hold the front tire steady.

I should probably back up a bit here, Larry, and bring you up to speed on my brother Jordan, the human entrail. This is a kid who would have been better off raised by wolves, and he must know that, because he acts like he was. He's a teeny kid, with blond hair that looks like each follicle was installed separately and at a slightly different angle than the rest. If I didn't know better, I'd think Rod Stewart snuck into my mother's bedroom nine months before Jordan rocketed onto the scene. (Come to think of it, I *don't* know better, but that's another story, or at least another chapter.)

Anyway, picking up my brother from day care is an ordeal. I spend at least ten minutes listening to Mrs. Jackson tell me how far up the evolutionary scale he hasn't made it, another ten getting a detailed roll call of other day-care kids he's put on injured reserve, and fifteen trying to convince her that we *really* have applied for admittance to several other day cares and will contact her the *moment* we hear a word.

When I finally do gain his release, he won't get on the bike with me until I clothespin a playing card to the spokes, for that engine effect, and once we're moving I'd need at least seven bungee cords to hold him still. It's only about a mile back to our place, but no matter how hard I've trained that day, it's my toughest ride.

The story goes that my parents had Jordan to try and keep their marriage together, which is a real joke because Dad split the same weekend Mom was in the hospital having him. Mom had been secretly attending a woman's support group for more than a year to help her deal with his controlling ways, and she must have been ready to graduate because she was so thrilled at finding him gone, she threw an enormous "divorce bash" the very next weekend, and Dad's name was first on the guest list. Now my dad is not real fond of drawing attention to himself in potentially negative situations, but he'll always try to outdo you at your own game, so he showed two hours early with a professional photographer to take pictures for a divorce album to be kept at his bedside, so if he ever "woke up sweating in the middle of the night, worried that it was all a dream," he could leaf through it for proof.

Mom's crowning touch was to hire some newfound friends from a militant, over-forty, all-woman country-rock band called The Curse to play a drum-heavy variation of an old Tammy Wynette song which they called "Stand On Your Man" straight up at midnight, while she and Dad stood before the fireplace mantel taking sacred vows never again to darken each other's door without a court order.

That gives you a bit of an idea how far asunder those two put what God had joined. And I want to go on record right here, Larry, as declaring that it didn't surprise or disappoint me one bit, because I have never been able to imagine why two people as different as my mom and dad would allow themselves to be seen on the same street corner, much less try to spend their lives together. Plus—and I'm sure I'll get into this later—that there house weren't big enough for him and me.

That's as frivolous as I've ever seen my father, and I think he played it out because he didn't want to look bad in the face of my mother's growing strength, but that's basically the remains of the family my brother Jordan was born into. He thinks every kid has two houses and two sets of clothes and a duplicate of every toy and parents who'll give their kid any damn thing he wants to win him over from the other. The little turd is lucky to have a big brother to keep him in line. I'm amazed at how much Dad will put up with from him before sliding back into his old ways, and stashing Jordan in his bedroom. But maybe that's just me singing the Firstborn Male Child Blues.

There's more to October 10, Lar, but I don't have time to write it down right now. Catch you before sacktime.

      Ever your loyal subject,

      Beau-re-gard

Sixth period—the last of the day—is Lion's class preparation hour, and normally he drives across town to the university, where he has coached the swimming team the past four years, to prepare the afternoon workout. Today he hangs around school, knowing Keith Redmond also has sixth-period prep and that he can probably catch up with him in the teacher's lounge before Redmond heads for football practice.

Lion finds him relaxing on the couch behind the sports page of the *Spokesman-Review*, and drifts to the counter next to the sink, pouring himself a cup of coffee. It's a prop—he's not about to give himself the opportunity to compare it to Dr. Stevens's coffee. He moves to a chair on the opposite side of the coffee table from Redmond, who has yet to look up. Lion arranges the words carefully in his head, willing those least offensive to the surface. "Could I talk with you a minute, Keith?"

Redmond hesitates, obviously annoyed, then slowly lowers the paper. "Mr. Serbousek."

"I hate to interrupt," Lion says, "but I just need a minute."

"Is this about Brewster?"

Lion nods. "Yeah, as a matter of fact, it is."

Redmond's face disappears back behind the paper. "Save your breath," he says. "If I had my way that kid would be out of school for the remainder of the year."

"Jeez, it's only October."

"The kid has no respect."

Lion is quiet. He's heard that terminology all his life, usually directed at himself, and he knows it's misnamed. He respects many things, as certainly Bo must, but that's another issue and this isn't a philosophical discussion. If it were, he certainly wouldn't be having it with Keith Redmond. "Maybe that's not the point."

"I don't know why you always take up with the riffraff," Redmond continues. "It does those kids no good to have an adult entertaining their ideas. It only makes their lessons harder in the long run. I know you new guys mean well, but if you stay in this business as long as I have, you'll learn that coddling kids doesn't make them strong."

Right, Lion thinks. Humiliation makes them strong. "Look," he says, "I don't want to coddle Brewster, but this kid has some talents lacking in the rest of the riffraff I take up with. I don't think it helps him to be at war with the school all the time, and I don't think it helps us, either."

"Brewster declared this war," Redmond says. "I've been doing things the same for more than twenty-five years, and I'm not going to change because one kid can't respond, I don't care what his talents are. He had his chance to show those talents on the football field, and he quit. All he has to do now is get with the program. And in case you don't agree with that assessment, Mr. Serbousek, you should know that his father does."

Lion has learned the hard way that there's a time and place to cut your losses and a time and place to make a stand. He knows Redmond is contemptuous of his way with kids and his beliefs in general—not to mention his suspicions regarding Lion's life. At this moment seniority and arrogance give Redmond the upper hand. "So what does he have to do to get with the program?"

"I've told Dr. Stevens he can return to my class if, and only if, he is enrolled in the anger management group Mr. Nakatani provides for those in need."

Lion breathes deep. "Do you know what kind of time that requires?"

"Better now than when the problem is completely out of control," Redmond says, returning to the sports page. He glances up again briefly. "He can use the time he would have been on the football field."

Lion rises and pours his coffee into the sink. "Thanks for your time." He walks briskly into the hall, then jogs toward the parking lot, muttering unkind things.

Keith Redmond drops the newspaper onto the coffee table and shakes his head. These new guys come in all fired up, ready to set the educational world on its ear, certain they have new ways to stimulate kids who can't be stimulated. It takes time, but they all learn. They learn or they get out. When they've been in the business as long as he has . . .

Still OCTOBER 10

Dear Mr. King,

Here's a dilemma for you, Lar. Mr. Serbousek called tonight to ask if I wanted to go eat some pizza with him. Now, I've been around enough to know that meant bad news, because adults don't massage your stomach unless they're about to put the squeeze on your psyche. (There's a theme for an adolescent self-help manual. I'll call it *Teens Who Trust Too Much*. But let's get this one published first, okay?) Anyway, I pedaled over to Gatto's, Clark Fork's premier—and only—pizza place, because, whether I let him massage my stomach or not, my psyche would still get scrunched.

"What do you think of Mr. Nakatani?" Mr. S said, once we'd ordered a large Gatto's Surprise and sat down to wait with his beer and my Coke.

I said, "He's okay, I guess. I hear he's pretty far out there, but I've never taken a class from him. I signed up for shop class in junior high, and after the first week the teacher promised me an A if I'd build model airplanes for the rest of the semester and vow to remain at least ten feet from any tool that plugs into the wall. Since then I've stayed as far from Industrial Arts as I can without going to home tutoring."

He laughed. Then he said, "Speaking of home tutoring . . ."

"Oh, jeez. Really?"

"Don't get excited. It's among the choices. That's why I asked you about Mr. Nak. You know that anger management group he runs before school?"

"You mean his gang of future lifers?"

He laughed again. "Hey, some of my favorite kids are

sentenced to that group. But yeah, that's the one."

"I gotta go to that?"

"No, you can do four weeks of home tutoring with Mrs. Conroy if you'd rather. Then come back on probation."

"Until the first time I cross Redmond again. Shit." Now Larry, I gotta tell you what kind of choices I was being offered here. I took Geography from Conroy as a freshman, and the woman can flat put you to sleep. And the second your forehead splats onto the desk, she calls your parents; has a phone right there in her room. Next thing you know you're wiping the drool off your chin and she's standing over you with the handset saying your dad wants a word with you. My biggest worry about home tutoring is that she'd then know where I live. On the other hand, there's the Nak Pack. That's what they call it, no kidding, Larry, and if you wanted to put a major crimp in Clark Fork's future crime wave, you'd call an air strike down on their next meeting. Man, I wish they still just paddled your butt when you screw up; you know, let the vice-principal take a few slap shots at your ass to even the ledger. Besides, I manage my anger well enough. I can get a little out of hand at times, but I really don't think I belong in that group.

I asked Mr. S what would *he* do.

"First, I'd quit calling Mr. Redmond an asshole," he said. "Then I'd go with Mr. Nak. He's a smart man, Bo. He knows some things you could use."

I said, "I'm not worried about Mr. Nak. I'm worried about his band of thieves. I mean, I'm not that bad."

Lion said, "Close your eyes."

"What?"

"Trust me. Close your eyes."

I closed my eyes.

"Imagine a screen," he said. "Like a movie screen." He waited. "Got it?"

"Got it."

"Now picture a vertical line drawn exactly down the middle."

"Okay."

"On one side, envision Mr. Nak and his murderous thugs, guns and knives evident, fangs bared. On the other, picture Mrs. Conroy any way you want to."

I said, "When's the first meeting?"

Ever so humbly yours,

John Dillinger

CHAPTER 3

Dear Lar,

It's straight up midnight, and I just popped out of a nasty dream like someone detonated an M-18 in my garbage can. I remember back in Mr. Baldwin's Freshman English class, we were studying comic and tragic elements of Shakespeare, and Baldwin said any great piece of literature contained both. Since I barely understood a word the thee-and-thou master wrote, I had decided his work contained no comedy at all, and the tragedy was that we had to read this shit. Knowing that would never do on an exam, I asked for some definition. Baldwin said, "It's tragedy when it happens to you and comedy when it happens to someone else," and he went on to explain how the two are often the same, and they're distinguished by the manner in which any given incident in a story is presented. I guess if this autobiographical quest for Ironmanhood is to be truly great literature, which you no doubt believe it is or you wouldn't still be with me, I should come forth with a little of the tough stuff.

Since this evening when Mr. S told me I have to go to Mr. Nak's anger management group, I've been trying to understand why I'd rather snort number-five salsa than set foot in that room tomorrow morning, and I think it might be because of something Mr. S said when we were walking out the door of Gatto's; something I conveniently omitted from my last entry. He said, "Bo, Redmond may or may not be an asshole, but your anger comes from your life." I asked what he thought was wrong with my life, and he said he wouldn't be the one to know that. I would.

I didn't give it much more consideration because adults aren't always on the money, even righteous dudes like

Mr. S, but then I get this shotgun wake-up call at high midnight. I have this dream a lot: I'm standing by a huge steel door, intent on closing it in absolute silence. My father looms over me, hands on his hips, eyes blood red like some kind of special effect. (That's how my dad always looks right after he wakes up.) I push the door so carefully it doesn't even creak, and get it *almost* shut without a sound. Dad glares; he's *huge*, way bigger than in real life. I handle the doorknob as if it were filled with nuclear waste. Just when I think I've done it, the latch clicks like a shot put dropped in an echo chamber and I freeze, staring back into Dad's scowling eyes, and try again. Tonight I woke up on my third failure, my bedding crumpled on the floor, sweat pouring off me like early spring runoff.

I know exactly where this dream comes from, Larry, but that doesn't stop its effect on me. See, my dad is a man who lives by his schedule. Before their divorce, Mom left a cup of soup and a sandwich (tomato soup, tuna san) on the kitchen table each day. Dad came home from the sporting-goods store (which he owns) precisely at twelve, scarfed down lunch in five minutes, and napped the rest of the hour. Waking my father from his noontime nap was like castrating a wolverine with hot tongs and a dull knife.

One Saturday in September when I was nine, my sister Kathy, who's three years older than I am and off on her own, was playing on the front lawn with me, on the side of the house farthest from my parents' bedroom, where the giant slept. It was hotter than the hubs of hell outside, and Kathy got after me with the sprinkler hose. She bore down as I streaked for the house, my jeans soaked, my T-shirt stuck to my body like cellophane. I reached the front door at full speed, shrieking as I kicked it open and slammed it hard; safe, momentarily forgetting I had ventured into the cave. I remembered the dragon at the same instant I glimpsed that spot where his dark slacks touched the top of his black wingtips. The crease was perfect, the shoes nicely shined, and I was in deep, deep shit. I brought my gaze slowly to his simple silver belt buckle, past the green alligator on his gray knit shirt to the deep bedsheet crease running vertically the length of his cheek, and into those bloodthirsty eyes.

"What in *hell* do you think you're doing?"

"Kathy was—"

He roared. "I asked you a question!"

"I was running from—"

He held his wrist in front of my nose. "Do you see what time it is?"

I looked at the watch . . . quarter to one. "Yes."

"Do you know what that means?"

"Yeah, but Kathy was—"

"DO YOU KNOW WHAT THAT MEANS?"

Even at nine I could take only so much confrontation before locking down. I have forever hated feeling small and helpless. I gritted my teeth and said, "Yes."

"You will stand here and open and close this door, *quietly*, ten times."

"But Kathy—"

"Did you hear me, young man?"

I stood ramrod straight, Larry, and the tension in my neck and jaw drew tighter than a bowstring. Airy dots danced before my eyes as I opened and closed that door so painstakingly its hinges didn't squeak once. With each repetition, the latch clicked into place with silent precision.

Nine times.

On the tenth, I swung the door wide as the mouth of a crocodile in your toilet at the moment you squat, and slammed it so hard four windowpanes cracked from top to bottom.

Dad stared in disbelief.

I stared back in true belief.

"I'll check with Mr. Jarms down at the hardware

store," he said. "You'll receive the bill for those within two days."

"Fine."

"Now open and close it gently twenty times." Dad's mouth barely moved as he spoke, and his intensity hung over me like wet fog.

I said, "No."

"Excuse me?"

"No."

"I'll beat your butt till your nose bleeds."

I turned around and offered it up.

Dad and I had reached our first clear impasse. The one thing he wouldn't do was hit me, and the one thing I wouldn't do was open and close that door one more time without ripping it off its hinges. Looking back, I'm still astonished at the flood of humiliation and hatred washing through me as I stood facing him, the field mouse before the hawk. I still don't understand it completely, Lar, but one step backward was the abyss, and I made my nine-year-old stand.

A bill from Jarms's Hardware lay on my pillow when I arrived home from school the next afternoon—thirty-eight dollars and seventeen cents, installed—and my allowance dried up like a creek bed in Death Valley until it was paid in full.

And my isolation began. Dad sat the family down at the dinner table that evening and announced that as long as I wasn't willing to respect the rules in his house, he felt no obligation to me other than the provision of basic food and shelter. Until I was willing to open and close that door gently twenty times, I would come home directly from school each day, extracurricular activities being a thing of the past. Mom was to serve my meals in my bedroom, one helping from each of the three basic food groups and no more; desserts went the way of extracurricular activities. She was forbidden (a word she loudly eliminated from the family vocabulary the night of

24

the divorce bash) to wash or iron my clothes; I would do that at a designated time each week. My homework was to be done in my room, and I would not be invited to family activities, including watching TV, a privilege reserved for "contributing" members.

I disappeared. For almost seven months I ceased to exist. Dad persuaded Kathy that if I refused to respond to discipline, my life would amount to garbage; that she could help me by respecting his embargo absolutely. This shit was for my own good. He forbade conversation with me other than what was utterly necessary.

Mom secretly urged me to apologize and perform the ritual openings and closings of the magic door, but I wasn't sorry and would happily eat a bowl of live bumblebees before I'd give that son of a bitch the satisfaction of bringing me to my knees. So she watched helplessly as I fell into a monotonous after-school grind: nap, eat, nap, homework, read, sleep.

Through each of the first twenty-four days of December, I glanced sideways at the Christmas tree as I passed through the kitchen and living room on the way to my bedroom, noting the scarcity of presents, and I truly believed my heart would break. So be it. In the wee hours of December twenty-fifth, I lay on my bed reading a Popeye comic book while my parents and sister opened their gifts less than four feet on the other side of the wall, and I felt a cold, stainless steel cage close over that heart. I vowed he would never win.

Two days after New Year's, my mother came into the bedroom and asked how long I was willing to let this go on.

I gritted my teeth, blinked back the tears, and said, "Forever."

She begged me. "Please, Bo. Your father won't budge. You know how he is. I *hate* this."

I said, "He can go to hell," and she slapped my face.

I said she could go to hell, too.

It was Easter Sunday when Dad finally came into my room and said, "You may rejoin the family now." Nothing more was said at the time, at least not to me.

It was the nature of my father's power over us that no one outside the family had an inkling of my interment. Even as we stood locked in our struggle, I knew family business was no one else's, and never thought to call for help. I waged my war alone. I don't think I've ever forgiven Dad for the time he stole, but though we've had plenty of raging conflicts since, he's never taken me on like that again.

But now I'm real nervous about where things are headed, Lar. I do *not* want to join Nak's Pack, and not just because it's filled with desperados who've stashed body parts in the dark corners of their basements, either. I'm afraid that story's the kind Mr. Nak will want to hear—there are plenty more where that came from—and even *thinking* about telling them in a crowd puts a hole in me. Plus, as angry as I get at my father, something in me wants to protect him from the outside world.

Mr. Nak is one of those guys who knows stuff, Lar. I mean, *knows* stuff. He's a little Japanese guy—you probably figured that out from his name—from Texas. He talks like Slim Pickens and dresses like his fashion guru is the Marlboro Man. I'll bet he doesn't weigh more than a hundred-thirty-five pounds and he couldn't be five and a half feet tall, but peculiar as he may be—which is pretty peculiar if you believe half of what you hear—he's got this *confidence*. I don't know about you, Lar, being a guy who has interviewed Dustin Hoffman and Cher and G. Gordon Liddy without breaking a sweat, but guys who can look inside you scare the hell out of me. You never know when they'll come out and say what they see. I can't tell you how much I'm afraid of looking bad. The loons I know in Anger Management aren't afraid of anything. Those guys will divide up my belongings if they see what I'm really like. Being uneasy in front of people makes me feel out of control, and when I feel that way I do things I would never do when I'm okay. More than anything, I hate feeling foolish.

Like with Redmond. Hell, I knew I had two suspensions. I knew what happens when you get three, and I knew I was mixing it up with the one guy who'd go out of his way to give me the third, but when he started repeating my name like some ridiculous mantra, I felt every kid in the room staring at the humongous wuss inside me, and it was exactly like that day with my dad; I didn't care what Redmond did to me.

Not that school itself is a big deal, but I really do like Mr. S's Journalism class, and I need to graduate. Plus, I've been lifting and working out pretty hard and I'm not looking that bad—still on the scrawny side, maybe—and I think there's an off chance I might be able to snag me a girlfriend if I could stay around long enough to build up a little rep. I don't want to lose all that.

Another thing: When I get freaked and go off on a guy like Redmond, I usually feel okay *inside*, even though I know big trouble is coming, because Redmond really is an asshole and I don't care whether he likes me or not. But the minute the word "asshole" spills over my lip, I know he's got me. Though my diagnosis may be correct, all anyone sees is a bozo out of control. Afterward, I'd do anything to keep them from seeing that.

Even worse, I trash people I care about that very same way when I start looking bad, and when I get rolling I can't stop, don't want to stop. I do it with Mom all the time, and I did it with the only girlfriend I ever had, so far. When it's over, I feel stupid and ashamed, and I don't think there's a feeling worse than that.

Enough. There are no answers in life, and I'm afraid I'm making a case for attending Mr. Nak's group. Besides, I need my sleep. Mr. S said I could work out with the university swim team if I'd show up at five o'clock in the A.M., and that comes early. Thanks for listening, Larry.

You're a good host. After you've made me famous with
this masterpiece, you ought to think about being a shrink.

Outta here,

The Big B

"Man, what's *he* doin' here?" Ian Wyrack nods toward Bo
standing chest deep in the university swimming pool, gasping
for oxygen after the last swim in a set of twenty hundred-yard
sprints. "He isn't on the team. Hell, he isn't even enrolled here.
Aren't you that high-school punk whose picture was in the
paper for that triathlon crap? Wants to be an Ironman or some
shit?"

" 'Punk' and 'Ironman' in the same sentence would seem a
contradiction in terms, Ian," Lion says from the deck. "Besides,
I counted eight of those repeats in which this high-school punk
kicked your butt."

Wyrack pulls himself out of the water, his triceps bouncing
on the backs of his arms like tennis balls, pectorals dancing. Bo
glances up, then quickly away, thinking, This guy is Terminator
III.

"Shee," Wyrack says, "I dogged those."

"You sure you want me to know that?" Lion asks, and the
shrill blast of his whistle ricochets around the walls of the pool
house. "Line 'em up!" he hollers. "By his own count, Wyrack
dogged eight of those! Help him out, guys; let's do those eight
again!" To a man, the small team of nine swimmers groans.
"Way to go, Wyrack!" "Nice job, Wyrack!" "Hey Wyrack, keep
it to yourself!"

Wyrack kisses his knuckles as Bo drags himself from the
water. "You're meat, Ironman."

"I'll assume you're dogging any repeat Brewster wins," Lion
says, his eyes following the second hand on the giant workout
clock above Lane Four as it drifts toward twelve. He moves
behind Bo five seconds before the start whistle. "A true Ironman would take that as a challenge," he says in a low voice.

"See how long you can keep these guys in the water. I'll let you out a few minutes early to get to Mr. Nak's group. You'll be gone before Wyrack has dried off." He blasts the whistle.

Sixteen hundred-yard sprints later, Wyrack finally touches the wall a tenth of a second ahead of Bo for the eighth time to end that workout segment. He is without sufficient oxygen to predict Bo's short lifespan aloud, but draped over the lane divider, sucking air like a tropical depression, he points a finger at Bo's heart.

At the same moment Lion glances at his wristwatch. "Brewster, you're outta here, man. Gonna be late to your early morning class. Thanks for giving us a push."

Bo hauls himself once more out of the water, refusing to look back in the direction of the groans.

Don Sheridan, the head janitor, bangs down the panic bar with his broom handle from the inside on the side entrance door, allowing Bo to enter the school building. "Bad boys is down in thirty-two," he says, pushing his sweaty Notre Dame baseball cap back on his crown. "Best hurry if you want a good seat."

Bo thanks him and starts down the long, unlighted hallway.

"How'd you get yesef in with that bunch?"

Bo turns. "Just lucky, I guess."

"Well," Don says, "that kinda luck, I wouldn't spend my allowance on lottery tickets. I know you—Brewster, right?—an' you're trouble, but you ain't that kind of trouble."

"Tell Mr. Redmond that."

A look of acknowledgement crosses Don's face, and he laughs. "Naw, that's okay. Redmond's a prick. First few years I done this job, had this little rat-lookin' dog I couldn't get housebroke. Used to leave him in Redmond's room while I cleaned the rest of the school. I'd still be doin' that if Redmond wouldn't a' started blamin' the kids. Bunch of 'em he thought done it got a three-day vacation. Hell, I ain't said a word to him since I dropped outta tenth grade. That there's a philosophy you might wanna adopt."

Bo doesn't argue. Don's been head janitor almost fifteen years and most of the students like him, though they have dubbed that portion of his ample posterior that peeks over the back belt loops of his low-slung jeans "the crack of Don." Don has seen a lot at Clark Fork High over the years that he has kept to himself, as if he knows the kids need at least one person over twenty-one on their side.

Bo gazes into room thirty-two with great apprehension. It is too much like his dream. Mr. Nak sits cross-legged atop the teacher's desk, with more than a dozen students, ranging in age from fourteen to nineteen, seated in a circle. Anger seems heavily male, as there is only one girl—the one he saw working out in the university weight room. Small world. All eyes fall on him in the doorway.

"Aha," Mr. Nak says in his slow Texas drawl, "everbody present and accounted for." He motions Bo to the one empty chair in the circle.

Bo breathes deep, and moves slowly toward the seat.

OCTOBER 11

My dearest Larry,

I think anyone who wants to get his temperament firmly under control should stand in the doorway to Mr. Nakatani's anger management group for about sixty seconds or so, and let the member felons cast their gaze upon him. What you say to yourself at that moment goes something like this: Dear God, I will never again raise my voice in anger against anything—living or dead—on your sacred planet, I will besmirch not one of your creatures no matter how disgusting, not even my brother or his puppy-mill cocker spaniel who watches television seven hours a day and gets so excited when he snatches food off your unattended plate that he pees all over the floor; and I will eat leafy green vegetables as the main course of every

30

meal with a smile on my face if you will please, oh please, just turn back the hand of time to the moment I did whatever I did to get me here and make me be a good boy.

It seems God doesn't answer your prayers without first taking them under lengthy advisement, and I didn't have time for that because Mr. Nak motioned me to my place among the thieves and murderers.

He said I must be Bo Brewster.

I said, "Yes sir."

Two or three of the inmates snickered, and Mr. Nak said that was because they hadn't heard anyone called "sir" since they were last in juvenile detention.

Mr. Nak said the group was a little short on manners, as I could probably tell, but that everyone would introduce themselves shortly. "Shuja," he said, nodding toward the only black kid, "why don't you tell Bo how things work in the early mornin' here on the ranch?"

"Why, I'd be right proud to," Shuja said. He's a big, strong, good-looking kid with a wide-open face that looks like he never gets mad. "First, some teacher who don't like your black ass just 'cause it's black tells you you got a 'tude, and you best be gettin' here to Mr. Nak's early mornin' 'tude-fixin' class or you won't be comin' back to school, in which case you won't never get no diploma, in which case you won't never get no job, in which case you're gonna end up in prison like your older brother done. Then, since you can't be lettin' no midget shiny-head algebra teacher be your fortune-teller, you say, 'Hey nigger, don' be predictin' *my* life 'til you got one a' your own,' and then they haul you away, and you show up here 'cause you wanna grow up to be a productive citizen of this here raggedy United States." He looked at Mr. Nak and smiled. Most everyone else laughed.

Mr. Nak said, "That's pretty good, Shu, but I was hopin' for somethin' a little more general." He turned to this kid named Elvis, who everyone in school knows out of self-defense. Elvis is one of those guys who started

shaving in junior high, and then started using the straight
razor he shaved with to take everybody's lunch money.
He's a big guy, runs about two-thirty, I'd say; kind of fat,
but with plenty of muscle underneath, homemade tattoos
on all the parts of his body he could reach, and the
permanent expression of a pit bull about fifteen seconds
before a fight. "Elvis," Mr. Nak said, "you wanna take a
shot at it?"

Elvis just glared, trying to stare a hole in Mr. Nak.

"Guess not," Mr. Nak said, and turned back to me.
"Me an' Elvis are learnin' each other's body language," he
said. "Don't worry, Brewster, I'll find *somebody* who
knows what's goin' on here." He glanced around the
room, his gaze falling on the girl from the weight room.
"Shelly," he said. "Maybe you can pull me outta the mud
here." But Shelly said, "I don't feel like talking today, Mr.
Nak. Could you ask someone else?"

Mr. Nak said, "Anybody want to go for it?" and
everybody studied the floor. He smiled and looked back at
me. "Don't write my letter of recommendation just yet.
Only been at this a short while. I'll give you the
lowdown." He clasped his fingers around one knee and
rocked back on the desktop. "Everbody here is pissed off
about somethin', and everbody's done something while
they were pissed off that got 'em here. Now, what it is
that everbody's pissed off about is a secret. My job is to
find that secret. Any questions?"

I said nope.

"So make my job easy. What're you pissed off about,
Brewster?"

He caught me by surprise, so I said, "I'm not pissed off
about anything."

"Really? You takin' this course for credit?"

"Well, no."

"So how'd you get here?"

Shuja laughed and whispered loud behind his hand,
"Tell 'em you come in a limo."

I laughed back, kind of nervous like, and said, "I got into trouble with Mr. Redmond."

"What did you do?"

I hesitated, glancing around the room. Then, "I called him an asshole."

Spontaneous applause broke out, Lar, no kidding. Mr. Nak smiled. "Sounds like maybe you spoke for the masses. I think you're gonna fit right in here."

Everyone stopped clapping except this really weird-looking kid with long hair and a headband, wearing a University of Washington T-shirt so dirty it looked like a year-old dust rag, and bell-bottom pants. He just shook his head and chuckled and slapped his hands together like none of the rest of us was even there. "Called Redmond an asshole," he said, over and over. "Called Redmond an asshole. Whooeee. Called Redmond an asshole."

Mr. Nak said, "Okay, Hudgie, we heard him," and the kid jerked like somebody had slapped him back to consciousness, looked around kind of sheepishly, and said, "Called Redmond an asshole. That's a good one. Life sentence. No possibility of parole. That asshole Redmond will make sure of it." Hudgie didn't look like he needed anger management, Lar. He looked like he needed the space aliens who sucked his brains out to give them back.

"Tell you what," Mr. Nak said directly to me, "we'll get back to you. Why don't you just listen awhile, and see what you think?"

That sounded good to me. I'd had about all the attention I needed, because old Elvis never took his eyes off me once, and I got the feeling he'd soon be steppin' all over my blue suede shoes.

Mr. Nak turned to the rest of the group. "Anybody got anything they want to talk about?"

A kid named Joey raised his hand. He's one of the few regular-looking guys in the group—nice clothes, dark, kind of slicked-back hair, would be pretty good-looking if you could ignore the permanent scowl on his face. The guy looks like an Italian Mr. Yuk sticker. He said, "I got somethin'."

Mr. Nak said, "Go."

"We got a skunk in our house."

Mr. Nak said, "I'm assumin' you're not talkin' about your pappy," which got a few laughs.

"No, man, a real skunk. Comes in through the cat door."

Mr. Nak said, "That's interestin', but I was lookin' for an anger issue."

"Hey, man, this skunk pisses me off."

Mr. Nak shrugged. "Okay, so has he done his dirty deed in your house?"

"Not yet."

"What does he do?"

"He eats."

"That all?"

"Yeah, that's all."

"So why do you get all riled?"

"He's a *skunk*, man."

Mr. Nak looked at me. "Joey likes smoke and mirrors, likes to keep me off any subject that might get close to home." He patted his chest to indicate where home was, then turned back to Joey. "You got a plan?"

"Gonna shoot his ass. Got my old man's .22 and some buckshot load, and I'm gonna wait till I catch him outside and blow his ass to smithereens." He leveled an imaginary rifle at an imaginary skunk and said, "Bloooom!"

Mr. Nak rocked forward and smiled. "Yesterday, in one of his rare public outbursts, Elvis here demanded, 'How does anybody get out of this chicken-shit group?' I said 'anybody' needs to participate real regular in discussions, let the rest of us in on the parts of his life he—or she— don't want us in on, and respond to a few concrete assignments. You, Mr. Joe, get the first concrete assignment of the year."

"Yeah? What's that?"

"Leave the skunk alone."

Joey sat up straight. "You out of your mind?"

"That's been wondered more than once."

A titter ran through the group about then, Lar, and I remember thinking Mr. Nak sure is every bit as crazy as everybody says. I mean, he wants this poor jerk to invite a skunk to dinner.

Then Mr. Nak said, "Look, Joey, why is it you think the skunk ain't sprayed?"

"Nobody's pissed him off."

Mr. Nak said, "Hit 'er right on the head, pardner. An' accordin' to ever rap sheet I got on you—and there's one for ever week for ever teacher—you like to piss people off. For the next week, Mr. Skunk is goin' to represent Everteacher. It'll be your job to keep him all nice an' calm. Mess up an' you'll know it right quick."

Joey said, "Oh, man, are you kidding me?" Then he paused. "What about my old man or my old lady? What if they piss him off?"

"From what you said the other day, your parents could use a little work on their restraint, too. Tell 'em this is a family project. Kind of a Be Nice to Mr. Skunk Week."

"They ain't gonna like this."

"Tell 'em it'll get you through Anger Management quicker. An' it'll keep you all out of the principal's office."

"You might be getting a telephone call."

"Dial 1-800-MR-NAK."

You might think that cohabitation with a skunk is a bit of a strange assignment for anger management, Lar. I sure did, but hey, I'm new to this business. And I'm stuck with it because Redmond ain't budging. That's not without its irony, either, because it's pretty hard to imagine Redmond and Mr. Nak on the same planet, much less in the same school.

Gotta get a late-night run in, so I'm signing off. Don't worry, if things get too strange, I'll tone them down for the novel. We don't want any of that truth that's stranger than fiction in here, do we? I mean, is this a mainstream epic, or what? Play your cards right and you can make me fabulously wealthy.

Ever your loyal fan,

The Brew

CHAPTER 4

Lion pushes through the side door to the Industrial Arts wing of Clark Fork High School fifteen minutes before the bell signals the beginning of first period, to find Noboru Nakatani nearly disappeared beneath the hood of a 1964 Mustang. He resists the urge to announce his presence with a blast of the horn and gently drums the hood with his fingernails instead. "Hey, cowboy, what's happening?"

Nak backs out from under the hood, stepping down from the front bumper, wiping his hands with a grease rag. "Shoe Fairy had to give these boys a little hep with this engine," he drawls. "They like to tore it up yesterday, got so frustrated. I swear the young'uns in this class think ever tool's a potential hammer." Nak places his foot on the front bumper. "What's on your mind this mornin', Lion man?"

"Brewster show up?"

"Oh, yeah, he showed."

"What'd you think?"

Nak smiled. "I think he figured he come face-to-face with the Hole in the Wall Gang when he walked in the room, but he'll do all right."

"Think so? You think he belongs there?"

"You think he don't? Those kids ain't a whole lot different from any who've been roughed up pretty good. They're a little raw, but I'm bettin' they got all the same workin' parts as the fancier models."

"So you think Bo will make it okay?"

"I think he'll make it just fine. What is it you're worried about?"

Lion shrugs. "You know how some kids just get under your

skin? He seems hungry for something I've got, but I don't know what it is for sure."

"Best be findin' out," Nak says back. "You might have to step up."

"What do you mean?"

"I mean most kids ain't good at tellin' what they need because they don't know. Whenever we see it, that's the time to act."

Lion thanks him and disappears through the doorway leading down the long breezeway toward the main building: Best be findin' out. You might have to step up.

Nak sneaks back under the hood of the Mustang, humming "Tumbling Tumbleweeds."

OCTOBER 24

Dear Larry,

Getting a little testy there this morning, weren't you, Lar? Especially with the guy who said anyone who intentionally desecrates an American flag is a traitor to his country and ought to be treated the same as a person giving away national secrets in wartime. Your "freedom of expression" argument was good, and I liked your idea that people who *really* believe in the Constitution know that everybody's rights are protected, not just those who agree with us. What I'd really like to have in my own life, though, is that little button you push just before you say "Rest well," to end it for any caller who gets too stupid or belligerent for even your tolerance level. I would have called in, but by four-thirty in the morning "Larry King Live" isn't live anymore; it's repeated from yesterday. If I could have called, I'd have asked if you thought those rights of expression were for everybody, and I'm betting you would have said yes. Then I would have told you I'm a seventeen-year-old high-school kid and asked if you thought the Constitution held up for me, too. I'm kind of glad I couldn't really get to you, because I'm afraid you might have said what most adults say: that teenagers aren't quite *done* yet, that we're impulsive and adults intervene because we aren't ready to manage our lives. But in my four-thirty A.M. fantasy you gave a different answer that lent weight to my powerful need to express a thing or two to guys like Redmond and my dad. Who knows, maybe you would.

Thought I'd bring you up to date on the Nak Pack, because what's been going on the last few days messes with my head. After Mr. Nak told Joey to invite a skunk into the family fold, I figured the best way through was to be polite and keep my mouth shut. Then, about three or four months down the road, I would just tell Mr. Nak I never seem to get mad anymore, could he please tell Redmond I'm cured, and that would be that. But I don't think it's going to be that easy. See, Mr. Nak'll be talking about how anger comes creeping up, hoping you're not paying attention so it can trick you into something really embarrassing or degrading, and before you know it he's got you thinking about your life, or worse, *talking* about it. He keeps asking what seem like harmless questions, and it almost seems safe to answer them. Next thing you know you're ready to say something you thought you'd never tell anybody.

The other day he gave us this hypothetical problem. He said, "Okay, close your eyes an' pertend you're five years old." (Excuse the grammar and spelling here, Lar, but in case you haven't noticed, I write it the way Mr. Nak says it. Maybe it's a sign of prejudice, but listening to this long tall cowboy talk, coming out of a five-and-a-half-foot-tall Asian guy, is a kick.) Anyway, Shuja put up a stink when Mr. Nak said that, because in his world you close your eyes for *nobody*. What Hudgie sees when he closes his eyes can only be imagined, because the minicam in that guy's head is operated from a remote control long, long ago on a planet far, far away. So Mr. Nak said just do our best an' if things got too uncomfortable, it was okay to peek. He finally got us zeroed in on ourselves at our first day in kindergarten. Shuja felt obligated to tell us who-all's ass he had to kick just to start off even, because there's bigots everywhere, even in kindergarten, but Mr. Nak just nodded and went on. "Now imagine the person you been trustin' all your life, your momma or your daddy or whoever, has told you from the git-go that this color"— and he pointed to his green shirt—"is red. For five years nobody told you nothin' different about green an' red, so you start out your first day in school thinkin' this"—and he pointed to his shirt again—"is red."

Shuja laughed out loud and said, "Oooh, you gonna be scrappin' with all them homeboys tellin' you different than what your daddy tol' you," and I figured that was probably the point, and I peeked and saw Mr. Nak smile.

Then he said, "Let's drive our Jeep a bit farther down that rocky road. Let's say that same person you grew up with, who told you green was red, also told you that when you cross the street you best be lookin' out for all the forks and spoons speedin' by, because if you don't, they'll flatten you out like a dime on a railroad track."

Shuja said, "Oooh, shit" again, but Mr. Nak talked right on through him. "An' that same person, who you grew up with, an' who told you red was green an' cars an' trucks was forks an' spoons, told you anytime somebody asks your name, what they're really lookin' for is trouble, an' you best nail 'em before they nail you."

Even Elvis snorted a bit at that.

"What do you think your first day at kindergarten's gonna be like?"

Shuja said, "Gonna be a buncha ass whuppin'."

"Why?"

"Because ever time you open your mouth, you gonna be lookin' the fool, plus you're gonna light some kid up jus' 'cause he wanna know your name. Maybe even the teacher."

"Who you gonna be mad at?"

"Ever homey in the place."

Mr. Nak sat back. "Now why you wanna get all burned up at them? They're *right*."

"Yeah," Shuja said, "but they messin' with you."

"Are they messin' with you, or jus' tryin' to tell you the truth?"

Shuja snorted. "Tryin' to tell you the truth? You five years old, man. They be laughin' an' pointin'. Tha's the way with little kids. They won't be carin' 'bout no truth."

"Laughin' an' pointin'. Makin' you feel how?" Mr. Nak asked.

An unmistakable voice boomed here, Lar; for the first time in two weeks, Elvis speaks: "Like an asshole. So what?"

Mr. Nak pointed his six-shooter finger at Elvis's chest. "Right you are, pardner. Right you are. Just exactly like an asshole. An' that is my point. Twenty-five freshly scrubbed rug rats, wearin' brand-new sneakers an' got their hair all slicked down wet and flat against their heads, an' twenty-four of 'em know the right names for things. But not you. You gonna feel real smart? Don't think so. Gonna feel worth a damn—like bein' sociable? Un-dern-likely. Why? Because you're feelin' lower 'n a snake's belly in a wagon wheel rut, that's why." He pointed at me. "An' who you gonna be mad at, Beauregard, my boy?"

I said, "I guess I'd be mad at just about everybody."

"You're gonna be mad at yourself," he said quietly. "Mad at yourself for feelin' the fool, as Shu puts it; mad at yourself for *bein'* the fool. To keep that fact in hidin' you *act* mad at everbody else, because you got to hide the truth. You're mad at yourself for bein' somethin' less than ever other person in that room. You don't know why, but you are. An' I'll tell you somethin' else: The more of them thirty-five pounders you coldcock, the madder you'll be, because no matter how many of 'em you knock out, you're still the dumb one. The humiliated one. The out-of-control one."

Now that doesn't seem like it should be right, Larry, but it sure *felt* right.

Shelly, who I am fast falling in love with even though I'm meeting her in the next closest thing to a maximum-security prison, raised her hand.

"You don't have to raise your hand in here, Shelly. Everbody's got the same right to talk as everbody else."

"Mr. Nak, nobody told any of us red was green. At least they didn't tell me that. And nobody told me traffic was silverware."

"An' a lucky girl you are," Mr. Nak said. "But what about other things that were misnamed for you?"

"Like what?"

"Anybody ever tell you everthing's really okay when you're feelin' low enough to sniff whale dung? You think 'low' is one thing, they tell you it's another? Ever have somebody say you didn't really feel awful when you did? That you *shouldn't* feel bad when you were eatin' dirt? You think 'awful' is one thing, they tell you it's another? Ever have somebody tell you they were whackin' on you because they *loved* you?"

"Sure, that happens to everybody."

"Does that sound like the right meanin' for 'love'? How do you like it when that happens?"

"I hate it," Shelly said. "So what?"

"Why do you hate it?"

"I just do."

"Well let me tell you why *I* hate it," Mr. Nak said. "I hate it because I hate people tellin' me how I feel or how I'm supposed to feel; tellin' me what's inside me ain't real, because it makes the truth feel wrong, an' I gotta feel like a dumbshit for bein' wrong all the time." He pounded his chest. "This is *me* inside here. An' nobody but this Japanese cowboy gets to name that or put meanin' to it. An' I hated it a lot more when I was a kid because *now* I know why they're tellin' me that, but *then* I thought if I was supposed to feel one way an' I felt another, then somethin' was wrong with me. An' I hated takin' what was wrong with me out on the road for ever one to see."

Now he sat forward, like he was somehow looking each of us in the heart, and said, "An' like Shuja or Elvis, when somebody'd catch a glimpse of that weak part of me, I kicked his ass, or at least I tried real hard, because it made me hate myself an' that's the worst feelin' of all." He leaned even farther forward. "Y'all remember that. Self-hate is the *worst feelin' of them all*." He backed off a bit. "Feelins are real, folks. An' nobody gets to identify yours but you. Now what you *do* with those feelins is another thing, an' that's why we're here."

A lot of what he said rang true to how I felt while Redmond mimicked my name the day he booted me, Lar, almost as if he were trying to make me ashamed of who I was: I'm going to be enough of a friend, *Beau-re-gard*, to tell you that if you keep heading in the direction you're heading, blah, blah, blah. Is it not true, *Beau-re-gard*, that the day you missed my assignment, blah, blah, blah. I mean, the guy was trashing me, and it worked. I hated myself for not being smart enough to stay out of his way. I felt like my *name* was stupid, which should have had nothing to do with the original problem: that I hadn't done my homework.

I actually started to say that, but I'm not real comfortable in the group yet—part of me still thinks I don't really belong there—and besides, Hudgie started spinning out. "Worst feeling of all," he says, talking to whoever bounced up behind his eyelids. "Worst feeling of all. 'Hudge, you damn well know better! Gonna hafta do this for your own good. Doin' it for your own good.' *Sssssss! Sssssss!* 'Doin' this for your own good, Hudge.' *Sssssss!* Worst feeling of all. That's right, baby, worst feeling."

Usually everyone laughs when Hudge gets on a roll, but nobody laughed now. None of us even knew what he was talking about, but tears squirted between his clenched eyelids like water out the back of an ancient washing machine wringer. Shuja whispered, "Oooh, man! Homey's feelin' some *weak* shit." Then he looked up at Mr. Nak and said, "You best be bringin' him outta that, Mr. Nak," and Mr. Nak said, "Makes you uneasy, don' it, Shu?"

"*Damn* uneasy. Now come on, Mr. Nak, bring him on out."

Mr. Nak stood up and walked around behind Shuja and laid his hand real easy on Shuja's shoulder and said, "It's okay, Shu. I think ol' Hudge needs to dump off a few of them tears. Might jus' choke 'im to death if he don't."

But Shuja couldn't take it, and he leaped up and said, "Hey, man, I got to go to the bathroom, man, no shit, it jus' come up on me." Mr. Nak took his hand away and Shuja was *gone*. Left his shoes right there by his chair. Hudge hadn't heard a word, just kept making that *sssss*! sound and feeling the worst feeling of them all. Mr. Nak walked behind him and began massaging his shoulders, and when Hudgie finally opened his eyes, he looked surprised and disoriented to see us there. Mr. Nak dismissed us then, but he stayed there with Hudge, rubbing his shoulders and talking in that slow, easy voice.

I didn't notice how far under my skin that whole episode got when it happened, Lar, but it's been with me all day, even through a thirty-five-mile bike ride and a monster workout at the university weight room. Mr. Nak's take on anger touches me someplace deep, and what was going on with Hudgie was the real thing. Shuja knew it; hell, his shoes are probably still in the anger management room. And as crazy as ol' Hudge looked, something about him connected with me.

Hey, I'm calling it a night, Lar. Gotta get up bright and early—actually, *dark* and early—to face Wyrack, who I think is going to want a piece of me. I've been beating him pretty regular. Be cool on the air today. Let the loons have their say.

Ever your loyal fan,

The Mighty B

As he snaps his bicycle lock onto the bike rack in the parking lot adjacent to the Clark Fork University swimming pool in the early morning darkness, Bo glances up to see Ian Wyrack step out of his 1992 Geo Storm. Instinct tells him to run for it, but at least forty yards separate him from the pool entrance, and if Wyrack has to chase him down, he might be harder to deal with.

Bo notices two more swimmer's cars pull into the lot, and he pretends not to hear Wyrack's quickening footsteps closing the distance between them. Ten yards from the door he breaks into an easy jog, hoping to show no fear, but a vise clamps onto his shoulder. "You cost me some extra mileage these last few days," Wyrack says.

Bo turns, smiling. "Yeah, we're putting in some pretty fast repeats."

Wyrack's steel grip guides Bo to the solid brick next to the pool entrance, shoving his back flat against it. "Yeah, well, maybe a little too fast," he says. "Coach can't get it out of his head that I'm dogging anytime I don't kick your ass."

Hey, you're the one who said it first, asshole, Bo thinks. "Yeah, I guess he does."

Three more swimmers approach and Bo anticipates serious carnage. "I'll warn you once," Wyrack says. "You better not give him any reason to think I'm dogging today, got it?"

Bo doesn't answer, glancing past Ian to determine the state of mind of the approaching swimmers, obscured in the predawn darkness. The first to reach them, a butterflier named Ron Koch, punches Wyrack's arm. "Hey, Wyrack, what's going on?"

"Nothing's going on, Koch. Go on in and get suited up. Tell

Coach I'll be there in a minute. Soon as I get some speed tips from the Ironman."

"C'mon, Wyrack. He's just a high schooler. Leave him alone."

"Hey, up yours, Koch. I'm just talking to him."

Koch persists. "Wyrack, I know you. Just leave him alone, man."

Wyrack releases Bo to face Koch square on. Ian is a full head taller and every bit as stocky. "Hey, Koch, unless you want a piece of me, get out of here."

"One of these days I might take you up on that. You're a real asshole, you know that, Wyrack?"

"Yeah. Keep your flattering remarks to yourself. Get out of here."

The other two keep their distance, following Koch as he reluctantly turns away, and in that moment of Wyrack's inattention, Bo breaks free to catch them. But Wyrack's hand grips the back of his neck like giant pliers, spins him, and slaps the side of his face so hard his ears ring. Wyrack pulls him close. "See this hand?"

Bo stares through him, anger crowding out his fear, boiling like lava.

"See this hand?" Wyrack says again.

Bo stares.

Wyrack slaps him again. "See this hand?"

Nothing.

Wyrack pulls him closer. "If your hand touches the wall before this hand touches the wall, *on one repeat*, you're gonna be seein' this hand up close again." He releases Bo's coat and walks slowly toward the locker-room door.

Ian Wyrack finishes ahead of Bo Brewster on a sum total of zero repeats for the morning workout.

"Good effort, Brewster!" Lion yells as Bo pulls his rag of a body onto the deck. "Hey, what'd you do to the side of your face? Get out of here or you'll be late for class. The rest of you, up on the deck. Let's knock off some sprints."

Bo refuses to look back at Wyrack's killer glare as he disappears into the locker room.

Lion emits a low whistle as he spots Bo entering his fifth-period Journalism class. "What happened to your face?"

Bo touches it tenderly and smiles. "Nothing."

Lion moves toward him. "Let me see that."

Bo pulls away. "It's okay. Really, Mr. S, believe me, it was worth it."

Lion moves Bo's hand gently away, examining the puffiness more closely. "Hey, I saw this at the morning workout, but it wasn't this ugly."

"Maybe it was the chlorine."

"Maybe it had just happened."

Bo smiles. "Maybe."

"Wyrack do this?"

Bo shakes his head. "Nope," he says. "It wasn't Wyrack. Nobody on the team. Really."

"You wouldn't lie . . ."

"Yeah, but I'm not. Really, Mr. S, let it go. No death, no foul, okay? I can take care of it."

"You beat Wyrack on every repeat today. . . ."

"I did, didn't I? It wasn't Wyrack. Don't be getting me in trouble with that caveman, okay?"

"This wasn't your dad."

Bo smiles again. "No. My dad leaves bruises on the inside."

Lion pulls back a step. "Look, Bo, I can't help you if you won't tell me what's going on."

"I don't need any help. If I do, I'll holler. Okay?"

"You're sure?"

"What're you, my mother? Jeez, Mr. S, it's a bruise. Barely even damaged the brain."

Lion nods, raising his massive hands palms out in surrender. "Okay, okay." He starts toward his desk at the front of the room and turns. "Your mother?"

"Only kidding."

* * *

"What happened to your face?" Bo's father glances up from the six o'clock news at Bo standing in the kitchen doorway.

"Bad genes," Bo says. "My dad's ugly."

"Keep it up, buddy. I'll even out your face for you."

"Judging from the way my day's gone, you'll have to stand in line," Bo says. "Where's the waste-oid?"

"In his room," Luke says, pointing over the back of his easy chair.

"Your idea or his?"

"He had it as I was about to get it." Luke nods toward the television set. "He got bored with world events. Everything okay at school? Are you back in class?"

Bo wrinkles his nose; the answers to those questions can't be covered with one word. "Yeah, I'm back in class."

"So I take it you're attending that anger management group."

"Yeah, Dad, I'm attending the anger management group."

"You know, you're lucky I'm not living at home with you anymore. You know what I've always said."

"I know what you've always said, Dad. 'Get in trouble at school and you're in twice as much trouble at home.' How come you never want to know what happened?"

"You know the answer to that."

"Yeah, but the answer sucks. You know the trouble with the 'get in trouble at school' lecture, Dad? It doesn't take *people* into account. If you'd take a look at just one of my school squabbles and say I might have had a point, it would be different, but that never happens and it isn't going to, because you never want to know my side. To accept your view of things, I'd have to believe in the divine rights of teachers."

Luke reaches for the remote as the credits roll over Dan Rather removing his earphone from behind the "CBS Evening News" desk, and mutes the sound. "Tell you what, buddy, it wouldn't hurt you a bit to start believing in that. This isn't about right and wrong, Bo, it's about obedience where obedience is due. You need to learn respect. What do you think it's like out in the real world? Do you think you're going to like every boss you have?"

"No, but all my bad bosses will have to give me money. Dad, I've been working two jobs for three years now; I've had three bosses at the newspaper who were alcoholic numbnuts, and I haven't even been reprimanded once. I don't think this is about respect. And I don't think it's about my future as a productive member of the work force."

Lucas palms the back of his neck. "Look," he says, "You've known the rules in Mr. Redmond's class from the start. I've talked with him personally about this, and we agree this all really started when you quit the football team. If you lived with me, it would have been taken care of back then. Mr. Redmond holds a position of respect and I would demand that you respect it, and that's that."

"Which is why I don't live with you, Dad." Bo feels the frustration of lost justice rising in his chest, a feeling that has, in the past, led to sorrowful actions. He has stayed in this conversation too long simply to walk away. The two of them came to some nasty verbiage over his quitting the football team back when it happened, but he's been practicing a different approach, thanks to some comments from Lionel Serbousek. "You know what? I do respect Mr. Redmond. I respected him when he taught me how to catch a football and take immediate evasive action, and to throw a solid block on a guy twice my size without losing my head, but that respect went down the toilet when he had to scream at me and question my manhood in front of the rest of the guys or the crowd at the football game when I didn't do it exactly right. I respect him for some of the things he teaches in English, but the second you don't do everything his way, he has to embarrass you. You know why I quit football? Hell, I was a starter—"

"You quit because you lack character, son. You were—are—a quitter."

Bo makes a loud buzzer sound. "Wrong, Dad. Hit the showers. I quit because I can't stand to be humiliated, and when Redmond gets pissed that's the only thing he knows how to do. I'm not the only one who believes that."

"That's one of the things you have to learn to live—"

Bo holds up his hand. "Wait. Lemme finish about respect. You know why I respect you, Dad?"

"You don't."

"C'mon, let me finish. I respect you because you teach me things. I've always loved how you never told me the answer, or took the tools away and did it yourself when I screwed up. You have patience when it comes to letting me learn things. You always stayed with me till I got that *I did it* feeling." He hesitates, then quietly, "It's the personal stuff that I don't respect."

Luke is silent, watching tears well in Bo's eyes.

"Remember the door, Dad?"

"What door?"

"The door that needed to be opened and closed twenty times before I could have my life back."

Luke bristles. "I remember the door. And if I'd had a brain in my head I would never have let you—"

Bo talks through his father's protest. "You don't teach a kid not to slam doors by humiliating him. I knew never to do that again the second I saw you standing there. Done. Lesson learned. But I lost respect when you were willing to let me live with that awful feeling inside me for seven months. How could I respect a guy that would steal a kid's Christmas over a stupid door?"

"If you're ever going to grow up, you're going to have to learn to deal with that awful feeling in a different way. Why don't you just get your brother and go? I don't need this aggravation today. Someday you'll see what I'm talking about and you'll thank me. Right now you're young, and you clearly have no sense of responsibility."

"Right, Dad," Bo says, feeling the heat rise again, crowding out the pain as the two of them drift toward that unresolvable point that reigns in each of their classic power struggles. "No responsibility. I work two jobs, go to school, transport the darling of the Brewster universe to and from day care each day and back and forth between his mom's and dad's places twice a week, and work out three hours a day."

"Other than school and transporting your brother, most of those things are choices," Luke says. "You do them because you want to. Responsibility is about doing things you don't want to do."

Bo takes a deep breath. "Well, I don't want to have this conversation anymore, so I'll take responsibility for ending it." He turns toward the back bedroom. "I'll get the turdburger and pedal him on home. Thanks for the lecture, Dad."

Luke picks up the remote control and waves his son away. "Get out of here," he says. "You always have to learn things the hard way."

OCTOBER 25

Dear Larry,

Remember that twelve-year-old kid who made national news suing his mother for divorce? I'll bet you do; every third caller had an opinion about it while it was going on. There was no sexual discrimination involved in that decision, right, Lar? I mean, there's no reason a guy couldn't do that with his dad? I think my father and I would get along much better if he didn't think he holds the pink slip on me. In her kinder moments, Mom says he means well, but I tell her it doesn't matter what he means if there's no way to please him and I have to feel like his rectal suppository every time we're together. He never once asked *why* Redmond and I got into it, what was going on inside me when I unloaded on him. It's probably a good thing, because if I'd been honest I'd have said I was feeling the same way toward Redmond as I feel toward *him* when he won't back off.

When I was eleven, just before my parents split up, my

dad paid me a hundred dollars to help his employees unload two truckloads of equipment overnight at his sporting-goods store, then set up displays for this big Halloween sale. My mother raised Siberian huskies back then—she still does—and I earned my allowance running the sire and the dam several miles a day. I should tell you, Lar, running Siberians is not an easy task for an eleven-year-old kid so skinny he carries rolls of quarters in his pockets in high winds to keep from being whipped off to Oz. The second you slip a harness on a Siberian, he assumes you're a sled and bolts for Nome. Commands like "Heel!" and "Wait a minute, goddamn it!" go unheeded by Siberians. To save time and mileage, I hooked the leash to a chain running between their harnesses and ran them together. I couldn't run on city streets because if they caught me off balance, they'd drag me right out into traffic, which there must not be much of in the Yukon because they have no sense of it whatever. Anyway, I usually ran the dogs on the service road beside the railroad tracks outside of town.

Dad arrived at the store about six-thirty that Saturday morning, just as we finished setting up the displays, and handed me a hundred-dollar bill from the cash register as I was leaving. The sun was just coming up over the wheat fields, and I thought I'd take Cooper and Deuce—Mom's dogs—for a short spin before passing out for the rest of the morning. Dad said to go straight home and put the money someplace safe, which is exactly what I intended, except I stuck it in the pocket of my windbreaker and forgot. At home I changed into my sweats, strapped on my weighted belt and wrist and ankle weights—which I always wore in an attempt to even the odds with those damn dogs—pulled the windbreaker over my sweatshirt and harnessed them up. Then I headed for the tracks, screaming at them to slow the hell down, which they translated into "Mush!"

About half a mile down the tracks I spotted a dark lump off to the side, and as I got closer, saw it was a person wrapped in blankets under a bush. You couldn't find a friendlier dog than Cooper, but you also couldn't find a more imposing one, at a lean, mean-looking eighty-five to ninety pounds, those eerie light blue snow eyes staring at you as if you were dinner. The guy saw us coming and shrank up under the bush, and I dug in my heels, because sure as guppies eat their young, these unruly beasts would want to go over and at least taste him. I reeled in the leash so I could get hold of the harnesses; sometimes I could get Cooper's front feet off the ground to equalize things. We were about three feet away when I accomplished that, and this poor guy stared out from his blankets in terror at what must have appeared to be a man-eating canine, standing almost five feet tall on his hind legs.

I said, "Sorry. They're friendly. They wouldn't hurt you. I know what he looks like," but he didn't say anything back, and I jerked the dogs on down the tracks.

The return trip was always easier because my little Deuce-Cooper was worn down from dragging me, so I had them under pretty good control when we came upon the man again, now awake and packed and walking slowly toward us. His hair was long and gray, his face brown and wrinkled as old leather. What appeared to be all he owned was wrapped in two blankets slung over his shoulder. I saw his socks through the toes of his boots, and his toes through the socks, another pair of which he wore on his hands. As we approached, he avoided my gaze and moved toward the ditch next to the road. The dogs were less interested now—though the man put off plenty of exotic smells—and as we jogged past, he caught me with a sideways glance that felt like a blow to my gut. It was the first time I recognized desperation, and though I couldn't put words to how I felt, I suddenly remembered the money in my pocket. Before I could even think I stopped, turned the dogs around, and went back. I placed the hundred-dollar bill in the sock on his hand and closed his fist around it; he never took his eyes off mine. I said,

"You should get something to eat, and maybe some shoes or gloves or something." He said nothing and the look in his eye never changed, and I backed away. When I was maybe twenty-five yards away I heard a long, anguished moan, and I looked back over my shoulder to see him standing, staring at the money in his hand.

I imagine that sound is heard sometimes when a mother finally gets food for her starving child, or when a dying AIDS victim is gathered in loving arms to let him or her feel the warmth of human touch that has so long been absent. I guess I'm saying that, even at eleven, when I hadn't seen fifty dollars in one place outside my dad's cash register, that sound was easily worth a hundred.

So, Lar, guess who didn't have a lot of time for my explanation of why my crisp new Ben Franklin hadn't found its way into my bank account at First Interstate. Tough guess, huh? Ol' Lucas Brewster was one pissed sporting-goods salesman.

"You did *what*?"

"I gave it to a guy, Dad."

"Well what did you *get* from this guy?"

I wanted to tell him, but I thought better. The cold and hungry man's cry rang clearly in my ears. "Nothing." I told him who I gave it to.

"You gave it to a tramp?"

"He was cold, Dad. All his stuff had holes in it. Cooper scared him real bad, and I couldn't see if he had any food or anything."

My dad palmed the back of his neck—his trademark gesture for times when his bonehead firstborn son tops himself in the startingly stupid move department—and walked to the other side of the living room. I thought about making a break for my room, but when L. Brewster palms the back of his neck and walks away, the only thing you know for sure is, he's coming back. "Beauregard," he said in that low, even tone that means you have offended his sensibilities in a criminal way, "do you know how many tramps there are in the world?"

The smartass part of me wanted to give him a number, but the survivor part of me pushed the smartass part of me on its smart ass. I said, "Probably a lot."

"What kind of job do you think you'll have to get if you want to give them each a hundred dollars?"

"Probably a pretty good one," I said. The hungry man's cry faded a bit, and I began to feel ashamed for being so stupid. Dad was right—a lot of people out there needed things. Still, if he had *seen* this guy . . .

He was quiet a minute more, then he said, "I guess you know you're going to have to repay that money."

He might have won me over if he hadn't said that. "What? To who?"

"To me. I didn't give you a hundred dollars to hand over to the first hobo that came down the pike."

"It was mine," I said. "I worked for it."

"I'm sorry, you're right," he said. "It was yours. So you'll repay yourself. That money was to go into your savings. You will repay yourself by earning a hundred dollars and putting it into your savings account."

Even at eleven, Larry, I had learned out of necessity how my dad argued—or at least thought I had—so I tried to help him make sense of it in that no-bullshit Lucas Brewster kind of way. I said, "Wait a minute. *I* lost the time and *I* lost the sleep and *I* lost the money. Even the way you think, that ought to be enough of a punishment."

He stood staring at me, slowly shaking his head. "Beauregard, that was a hundred dollars. If I thought you were capable of learning your lesson from what you lost, I'd let it go, but you have to learn the value of a dollar. What kind of father would I be if I turned you out into the world with your screwed-up sense of money?"

I retreated to the original passion of my argument. "But this guy didn't have—"

"This conversation is over, Bo. You show up at the store Monday after school, and I'll start you working to repay your debt."

"I have a flag football game Monday."

"Not anymore you don't. This is too important. You're going to learn to be responsible if it kills me."

"It's not fair! That man was—"

"This conversation is about the value of a dollar, son, and it's over."

I turned for the stairs leading to my room, knowing full well I was frustrated and angry enough to end up spending another seven months there if I didn't shut up, but I couldn't stop myself. Halfway up I turned around and screamed at the top of my lungs, "WHAT ABOUT THE VALUE OF PAIN?"

Dad's expression didn't change. "I'll teach you the value of pain, too," he said. "You just doubled it, friend. You'll earn two hundred dollars."

Better break if off here, Lar. That happened more than six years ago, and I'm sweating all over this paper telling it to you now. If I keep it up, I may have to run over to my dad's house and spray-paint peace signs all over his garage door. Catch up with you later.

Ever your loyal fan,

The King of Brews

CHAPTER 6

Ian Wyrack shouts across the parking lot outside Doc's Drive-Inn, located along Clark Fork's main drag. "Brewster! I wanna talk with you!"

"Talk to me from there!" Bo yells back. "I can hear you fine!"

"Your shit is in the street!"

"Tell me something new!" Bo feels relatively safe. It's Friday night, the lot is packed, and he's close enough to his mother's Blazer that if Wyrack makes a move, he'll have time to jump in and squash him flatter than a Monsters of the Universe trading card.

A soft voice in Bo's ear whispers, "Tell him to eat shit and die."

"Eat shit and die!"

Heads turn as Wyrack starts across the parking lot. The night is unseasonably warm for late October, and people who would normally huddle around the few tables inside Doc's are milling around their cars, their sound systems blasting rap and country and heavy metal and old-time rock 'n' roll with equal, and deafening, passion. Bo reaches for the Blazer's door handle, but slender fingers firmly grip his wrist. "Run now, and you'll run forever."

"I'm an Ironman. I can do that." He turns, Adam's apple to nose with Shelly, of anger management and weight-room fame, and his heart leaps.

"You *can* do it, but do you want to?"

Bo says, "What are my choices?"

She puts her mouth to his ear and whispers, "We can stand right here and kick his ass."

Bo pulls back. "We?"

"We."

Wyrack accelerates his pace across the parking lot. The decision must be made quickly.

"Okay," Bo says in a low voice, turning to face the oncoming rain of blows, "I'll kneel down behind him, and you push him over."

"Cute."

Sensing impending drama, a crowd begins to gather. Bo can almost feel the flat, hot palm of Wyrack's hand against the side of his face as Wyrack draws within feet.

"You want to say that again?" Wyrack sneers.

Shelly stands in Bo's peripheral vision, arms folded. Nothing like taking things too far to impress a woman. He glances at her in a fleet final effort to see if it's worth it. She's of medium height, with brown eyes and a short blond haircut that falls into place regardless of head movements. She isn't glamorous, but intriguing, with full lips, a petite, sharp nose, and a long, muscular neck. Her leanness is enormously sensual. So appearancewise, she's worth it, but what is she doing in Nak's Pack? Too late to find out now. "Eat shit and die," Bo says softly to Wyrack.

With the speed of lightning Wyrack's hand flicks out for Bo's face. With the speed of *greased* lightning Shelly's right arm blocks it as her foot sweeps his legs, caving them in at the knees. The side of her left hand catches him in the throat before he can hit the pavement, and she immediately stomps her crosstrainer Nikes onto his wrist.

"Bitch!" rasps from his throat as if his esophagus were coated with sandpaper.

"A bitch like you wouldn't believe," Shelly says, shifting more weight onto his wrist.

Bo stands astonished and paralyzed.

"Get off my arm, you bitch!" Wyrack yells. "You're breaking it! I gotta swim!"

"Apologize."

"You—"

She increases the pressure on his wrist. "Apologize," Shelly says again, almost matter-of-factly.

Wyrack grimaces, but his pride and the gathering crowd render him stoic. "Okay," he says without change of expression, "you're not a bitch."

"I know that," Shelly says. "Apologize."

"I'm sorry I called you a bitch."

"You made *my* day," she says. "Apologize to my friend."

Bo squirms. "No, hey, that's all right. I—"

"Apologize," Shelly says again.

"I'm sorry."

Shelly says, "For what?"

"Whatever I did, for chrissake!" Wyrack yells. "Get off my goddamn arm!"

"Not acceptable." Shelly stands down harder.

"I'm sorry for threatening you, Brewster, and for taking a poke."

Shelly stands off Wyrack's arm. "You didn't have to apologize for taking a poke," she says. "You never had a chance."

"Will you marry me?" Bo asks as he and Shelly slowly cruise Clark Fork's main drag.

Shelly smiles, and in the thick accent of a Georgia debutante, says, "Now why would I want to go and do a thing like that, Beauregard? What have you to offer for my hand?"

"You name it," Bo says. "I'm gonna need you by my side full time from now on. You're going to have to get up hours before daylight to escort me to swimming workouts, follow me endlessly on runs and bike rides, taste my food. . . . God, where did you get those Bruce Lee moves?"

"I'm going to be a Gladiator," Shelly says, staring straight ahead. "I don't have time to be your bodyguard."

"You're going to kill Christians?"

Dear Larry,

You have lots of interesting and far-out people on your show, Lar; ever have a Gladiator? There's a television show called "American Gladiators" that I've been watching recently because I think it will help me land a girlfriend: Shelly from Mr. Nak's anger management group, who has a fake student ID card just like mine for use at the CFU athletic facility. I didn't know this before, Lar, because she's pretty quiet in group and she doesn't dress to impress, but this girl is tougher than boiled owl. Now, a big-time talk-show personality such as yourself might question the efficacy of a human spear such as *my*self taking romantic interest in a young lady who could dismember me without breaking a sweat. She took out the CFU swimmer who's been dogging me so quick I would need slow-motion instant replay to describe it to you.

Anyway, whoever dreamed up "American Gladiators" hires these buffed-out men and women as full-time warriors to take on new contestants each week in highly physical games invented solely for this program. They have obstacle courses and bungee-bouncing madness and various other tests of strength and speed. The contestants are big and strong and in top shape, so the Gladiators have to be in bigger and stronger and topper shape, with names like Flame and Laser and Star and such, depending on whether one is a male or a female Gladiator. That's what Shelly is pumping up to be. And she's getting there, Lar. She's getting there.

So tell me what you think, Lar, of a guy whose masculinity quotient hovers just under triple digits, going out with a girl who can out-bench-press him by twenty pounds and fears no man? Kind of a nineties thing to do, don't you think?

Our first outing will be this weekend, to a Halloween

party. Great. She can go as Arnold Schwarzenegger, and I can go as his pet snake.

By the way, I heard you take on that caller this morning who said all homosexuals should be turned to pillars of salt. I had a strange reaction; I hate pompous buttwipes like that who are better than anyone who isn't like them, but I found myself divided. He kept saying homosexuality was a choice, and you kept asking exactly when he decided he would be heterosexual. (Of course, when he wound himself up so tight he was laying the radio waves flat, you said your customary "Rest well, sir" and left him stranded in Radio Neverland.) That's a disturbing question, Lar, because I've never thought of it like that. I don't know anyone who's gay, so I guess I don't know what I think.

> Rest well,
>
> The Brewski

"So how did you like visiting with my parents?" Joey asks smugly.

"I've rode happier trails," Nak says back.

"Told you you shouldn't have tried to make me kiss up to a goddamn skunk," Joey says. "Told you you didn't want to be around when my old man gets hot."

Nak smiles. "Actually, your daddy was downright tame compared to your mother."

"Yeah, well, my mother was home when the skunk blew. Dad was spending the night with his girlfriend."

Hudgie looks up in delight. "Skunk blew in your house? No kiddin'? Blew right in your house?"

"No kiddin', Hudge," Joey says. "My whole family's living in a motel right now. My folks are thinking about suing the school for damages."

"Sue 'em big time," Hudgie says. "Get millions. Bring the place to 'er knees. Close 'er down. Skunk blew. Right in the house."

Elvis snorts. "Man, this is bogus. I'm draggin' my ass out of bed in the dark every morning to listen to this shit? I thought we were supposed to be learning about our anger. This is turning into some kind of Bambi soap opera, guys invitin' skunks to dinner. I got no time for this."

Nak says, "So why do you show up?"

"'Cause I'm outta this bogus piece-of-shit school if I don't," Elvis says.

"Seems like that would be to your benefit," Nak says back. "Hard to see why you don't jus' hop off this miserable bronc."

"And have my old man turn loose on me? No thanks, Chinaman."

"I'm Japanese," Nak says, "and I've seen your old man. He ain't half your size soakin' wet. Unless he's packin' a shootin' iron, I don't reckon he'd have much chance of takin' you out."

"You don't know my old man."

"Maybe not," Nak says, "but this don't add up. There's more to this than you bein' scared your daddy's gonna hurt you. I'm bettin' he's got a bigger hold on you than that."

Elvis's entire body tenses. "Hey, maybe you don't know what the hell you're talking about."

"Wouldn't be the first time," Nak says, "but that don't usually stop me from talkin'." He expands his attention to include the rest of the group. "Tell you folks what. I call this here gatherin' Anger Management because that's what the powers that be want me to call it. But what it's really about is dealin' with whatever comes up, in a way that don't break you. If it's skunks, then it's skunks. If it's dads turnin' loose on you, then it's dads turnin' loose on you. But it all boils down to you. I'm not a man who's gonna tell you to go home and obey your parents or"—and he nods toward Bo Brewster—"your English teacher. I'm here to help you do what you do, then stand up an' own it in a way you can be proud of. Believe it or not, that'll give you a lot less to be angry about." He turns back to Elvis. "You can fight bein' here all you want, pardner, but when all the horses are in the corral, you gotta live with yourself an' how you respond to the people you think are makin' your life hell."

"Ain't nobody makin' my life hell," Elvis says.

"You're doin' that by yourself?"

"My life ain't hell!"

Nak says, "Eye of the beholder."

"Yeah, well, behold someone else's life. I'm sick of this shit."

"Your choice."

Bo is tentative. "Mr. Nak, how am I supposed to own what I said to Mr. Redmond in a way I can be proud of? I don't mind that I called him that, really, but I mind that I let myself that far out of control. I mean, you just don't go around calling your teacher asshole."

Shuja laughs. "Not to his face, you don't. Yeah, Mr. Nak, let's hear you teach this young sewer mouf how to be proud he called his teacher asshole. Now I could find plenty to be proud of, an' ol' Rock 'n' Roll here probably be all swellin' up in the chest if he done it, but this boy look like he come from a good home."

"I didn't say he should be proud of what he done," Mr. Nak says. "I said he should *own* it in a way he can be proud of. A man makes a mistake, he's got to be able to stand up and say so. That way he don't get so many of 'em stacked on his shoulders they weigh him down."

Shuja says, "So how he gonna own it in a way he be proud?"

"Name it an' claim it," Nak says. "He can say what he done and why he done it. If he thinks it was a mistake, he can say so. If he's sorry, he can say that."

Shuja laughs. "What if he ain't sorry? He get to go tell Mr. Redmond that? 'Mr. Redmond, my man, wish I was sorry I called you what you is, but hey, can't do it, homey.' "

"Probably makes more difference to the powers that he don't do it again," Nak says. "You don't have to say you're sorry to say you're gonna cut it out."

Shuja sits forward. "How come nobody make Redmond apologize for bein' an asshole?"

Nak laughs. "Eye of the beholder," he says. "One man's asshole is another man's toilet-seat cover. Sorry, Shu, you come to the wrong place if all you want is justice as you see it."

"Finish your piece on Yukon Jack's?" Lionel Serbousek stands behind Bo, who stares at an empty word-processing screen.

"Not yet. Can't get an angle. I don't think anybody at this school cares about some stupid triathlon."

Lion lays a hand on his shoulder. "Good journalism will make them care."

"I've been thinking about doing a piece on 'American Gladiators.' "

"*That'll* be an in-depth piece. What the hell is an American Gladiator?"

Bo quickly explains the concept.

"And you think people won't be interested in a triathlon?"

Bo explains why he wants to do a piece on American Gladiators.

"Tell you what, lover boy," Lion says, "you get me a three-part article on training for Yukon Jack's, and I'll consider letting you do a short piece on American Gladiators."

"You'll *consider* letting me do a piece?"

"Make Yukon Jack's a good one and American Gladiators is in."

"You're on," Bo says, turning back to the empty screen, staring a moment. Then, "I still need an angle."

"Do it from a Stotan angle," Lion says. "That'll win 'em over."

"What's a Stotan?"

Lion swells at the chest. "You're lookin' at one, lover boy. Find out what Stotan means, and you'll have your angle. Guaranteed."

CHAPTER 7

Bo gently pumps the brakes as his mother's Blazer approaches the stoplight at Browne and Sprague in downtown Spokane. Shelly sits relaxed, feet on the dashboard. It is Christmas Eve, and they are in town for last-minute shopping after a particularly intense workout at the CFU weight room.

"So what did you get me?" he asks. "Something pretty nice, I'll bet. Pretty expensive."

Shelly laughs. "You're right. I got you custom-made blow-up biceps that fit under your shirt so you won't be embarrassed to go out with me."

"Hey, I out-benched you today."

"Yeah, but you used both arms."

"Good thing I'm in Anger Management," Bo says. "Otherwise I'd have to jerk you out of the car by your coat collar and leave you bleeding in the snow." It has been an exceptionally hard winter all over the Northwest. Three to four feet of snow cover the ground, and snowbanks reach seven or eight feet in places where the plows have nowhere to dispose of it.

Shelly snorts and stares out the windshield. "Speaking of Anger Management, aren't you supposed to be getting out of there pretty soon?"

"One more week after vacation," Bo says, "but I don't know. . . ."

"You don't know what?"

"Between you and me?"

"Iraqi Gladiators couldn't make me break a confidence," she says. "*What's* between you and me?"

The traffic light turns, and Bo's tires spin through the intersection on the ice. "I'm not sure I want out of Anger Management."

"Brewski, we start before sunrise three days a week. Think of the extra sleep."

"I swim before group," he says. "Wouldn't be any extra sleep." Though the light is green at Second, Bo brakes for a heavyset man clad in only a T-shirt and jeans and sporting several days' stubble on his chin as he stumbles from the sidewalk into the intersection, oblivious to the traffic.

"Hey!" Shelly yells.

"Can't hear you," Bo says. "He's drunk. Besides, your window's rolled up." The man staggers in front of them, goosebumps and purple splotches of cold gracing his bare arms. He reaches the curb and Bo says "shit" under his breath, stomping on the emergency brake as he opens the door. Shedding his down jacket he jogs up behind the man, who flinches when Bo taps his shoulder. "Hey, man," Bo says, holding the coat in his extended hand. "Take this."

"Wha'?"

"Take this coat."

"Le' me alone." The man pushes the air in front of him weakly away.

"No, man, take it."

The man squints. "Whaddaya want? How come you're givin' me your goddamn coat? Whaddaya want?"

"I don't want anything," Bo says. "I want you to get warm."

"Git away from me!"

"Take the goddamn coat!" Bo yells, beginning to shiver in the single-digit Fahrenheit. Drivers backed up behind the Blazer honk as the light again turns green. Bo places the coat around the man's shoulders and hurries away, cranking the heat to high as he steps back into his vehicle. He watches in his rearview mirror as the man stands befuddled before sliding his arms into the coat and pulling it tight around his shoulders.

Bo says "ha!" in satisfaction, then "what?" in response to Shelly's silent stare.

"That was nice."

Bo shrugs.

"But I have a question."

"Shoot."

"What are you going to do for a coat?"

"I'm gonna buy a new one. I work for a living."

Shelly is quiet another moment, then moves across the seat and places her hand on Bo's leg and her nose next to his ear. "That was really nice."

Bo drapes his right arm over her shoulder and smiles. "It wasn't as nice as it looked," he says. "That kind of stuff pisses my dad off so bad it'd be worth it to freeze all winter."

DECEMBER 24

Dear Larry,

If I were mailing you this saga as I wrote it, you might have thought I dropped off the face of the earth, it's been so long since I've put pen to paper. I'll bring you up to date. Shelly's my girlfriend now. If you ever meet her, though, don't say I called her that, or I'll get Gladiator's knuckles for lunch. Shelly thinks "having" a boyfriend or girlfriend smacks of ownership and wants nothing to do with it. My mother agrees with her.

I said, "So what's to keep us from going out with other people?" and she doubled her fist under my nose and said, "*This* will keep *you* from going out with other people. The *choice* not to is all *I* need."

Hey, Lar, should a guy allow himself to be blackmailed by the brute force of a comely blond television warrior-to-be? And if so, how far should he let that go? My current thinking on the subject is yes, he should, and as far as she wants to go. I will welcome any opinion you might have that agrees with mine.

But there's more, and it's not good. My Sheena, Queen of the Jungle, has gotten me into some warm brown smelly stuff. Seems she got into a yelling match with Ian Wyrack, the mondo humongo swimmer from CFU, and told him to round up his two studliest fellow swimmers—

one to run and one to bike—to form a relay team so I could kick their collective butts in Yukon Jack's in May.

So I says to her, Lar, I says, "Are you out of your blood-vessel-constricted head?" and she says, "In every triathlon I've watched, the fastest individual has finished ahead of the fastest relay," and I says, "How many triathlons have you watched?" and she says, "One, but the first finisher was way ahead of the first team," and I says, "That, you cerebral behemoth, is because in almost every triathlon except Yukon Jack's the individuals *start* first, as much as thirty minutes before the relay teams."

She says, "Oh."

I say, "Oh," back.

"So sue me."

"There won't be enough left of me to sue you. The judgment would simply go to my descendants, of which I have none, because I'm too busy training like an Olympian to conceive any."

"Believe me," she says, "that's not the only reason you don't have descendants."

I prefer not to explore that further.

The good news is that Wyrack can only use guys from the swim team, and none of them can begin their training until swimming season is over in middle to late March, because Mr. S would kill them if they risked their lives running or biking on ice, or building muscles for any purpose other than torpedoing themselves through the water. The rest of the good news is that Wyrack is the only guy on the team who hates me enough to shove bamboo shoots under my fingernails, so he'll be the only one with the obsession of pushing me till I drop quivering and foaming at the mouth. I'm hoping the fact that the swim comes last in Yukon Jack's will keep my passion piqued enough to take him.

The bad news is that one of his guys is as much a cyclist as a swimmer. I can minimize his advantage by training all winter while he's sentenced to the water, but there's no way I can beat him. Still, that news isn't as bad as it could be, because, like I said before, Yukon Jack's is the only triathlon I know about that doesn't favor cyclists. What this means is that I'd better be in *monster* running shape, and training in these winter conditions is, in Shelly's words, the shits, especially when you're stumbling behind a team of two Super V-8 huskies with traction that makes your Nikes seem like skates.

No more time for talk, Lar. I'm off to train.

Later,

The Brew

Bo kicks the sides of his cross trainers against the doorjamb at the entrance to his father's apartment, turning the knob on the second knock. He hollers, "Hey, Dad" into the dark kitchen.

"Hey," his dad yells back. "Come on in. Merry Christmas."

"Same to you. Brought you some stuff."

Luke Brewster stands to greet his son as Bo appears in the doorway between the kitchen and living room, laden with food and gifts. Nothing in the decor of Luke's apartment hints at any celebration of the season.

"Damn, boy, where's your coat?"

It's Christmas; Bo chooses to fight another day. "Left it in the car." He places the gifts on the coffee table and glances around the bare room. "Thought you were going to get a tree."

"Naw," Luke says. "Maybe next year, when your brother's with me." He stares at the packages. "I wish your mother wouldn't do this. It seems like we've been apart long enough that she'd let things be."

"You know Mom. Can't think about anybody missing out on Christmas."

Luke's eyes go soft—something Bo seldom sees—as he reaches for the cup perched on the arm of his easy chair and takes a swallow. "Guess she doesn't know it'd be easier for me if she'd forget it," he says. His eyes snap back into focus and he raises his cup. "A little Tom and Jerry?"

Bo smiles and shakes his head, leaning his butt against the arm of the sofa. "No thanks, I'm in training."

"I wasn't going to add rum," Luke says. "I'll pour it virgin. Just some batter and hot water."

Bo appreciates the attempt at communication. "Okay. Sure."

When Luke returns from the kitchen, he hands Bo a steaming cup, raises his own, and says, "Cheers."

Bo nods and says "cheers" back.

They sit quietly a moment, sipping their respective drinks, and as he feels the weight of their silence, Luke says, "Beauregard, Beauregard, Beauregard. What am I going to do with you?"

Bo smiles and shrugs, realizing this probably isn't his father's first drink of the evening.

"We do go after each other, don't we, son?"

"We sure do, Dad."

"Why do you think that is?"

Bo shrugs. "Guess we both just want to be right."

His father sits back in the easy chair, nodding. "Maybe. Ever wish I'd just get off your back?"

"I almost never wish anything else."

"I'd like to, son. I really would."

"Well, don't let me be the guy that stops you."

Luke is quiet a moment, gazing into the gas log fire, looking lost. "But what kind of father would I be if I did that?" he says finally. "What kind of dad would just turn his kid loose in the world the way it is today?"

Sensing a window, Bo leans forward and says without malice, "You turned me loose when you and Mom split up."

"That may have been a mistake on my part. Turning you loose, I mean."

"You didn't have a choice."

"I could have fought for custody."

"It wouldn't have mattered. I was old enough to choose for myself and we hadn't had a decent conversation in years. I would never have stayed with you."

Luke's tone takes a harder edge. "If I'd had custody, you'd have stayed."

Bo feels the window closing and wills it shut. "You'll notice I haven't spent any more Christmases in my bedroom."

Luke's glare momentarily shoots daggers, then softens as he attempts to pry that same window open a crack. "That was a rough one for me, too."

Bo nods. "Yeah. 'This is going to hurt me more than it does you, son.' "

"That one may have."

"No way."

"Don't think you always know what's going on inside me, Bo. Sitting out in the living room in front of the tree that Christmas, opening our presents without you; it almost broke my heart. That one did hurt me more than it did you."

Bo continues shaking his head. "It *did* break my heart, Dad. If it had hurt you as bad as it did me, you wouldn't have done it."

Luke looks away. "Your turn will come, Bo. It will be interesting to have this conversation with you in ten years." He looks back into his son's eyes. "I'll tell you this, I never did anything to you I didn't think would help you in the world. I never did anything I didn't think would turn you into a better man."

For the first time in Bo Brewster's memory he watches a tear trickle slowly down his father's cheek, rest a moment on his chin to gather momentum, and drop almost lazily to the hardwood floor. He truly believes that. Bo literally aches to find some place of understanding with his dad, some place of peace, but before he can search, Luke's eyes snap again into focus, and his tone becomes matter-of-fact, as if he can tolerate only so much intimacy. "I understand you're about to be released from Anger Management. Learn anything?"

"How did you know that?"

"I keep in contact with the school. Hey, I'm still your dad.

Mr. Re—uh, one of your teachers told me you're about to be set free."

Bo slumps. "Yeah. You been talking to Redmond."

Luke waves a hand. "He was in the store picking up free weights for the off season."

"Oh," Bo says. It's possible.

"I hear you're taking on some kind of special challenge in your next triathlon," his father says offhandedly.

Bo feels off-guard. "You been reading my mail? Who told you that?"

"Heard you've got a new girlfriend, too. What's she like?"

"She's nice, Dad. I'll bring her around sometime."

"Heard she's on the beefy side."

Bo's pulse quickens with anger in response to the dig. It changes *so* fast. He decides to preserve what he can of Christmas Eve. "She's strong," he says. "She works out."

Luke leans forward, nodding. "To tell the truth, I'm kind of glad you're finishing up the anger management group."

"Why is that?"

"Well, you've probably learned your lesson by now, and I hear that Nakatani character has some pretty strange ideas. In fact, I heard he might have brought down a lawsuit on the school district. Something about a skunk."

Bo laughs. Though he thought it bizarre in the beginning, he has come to think of the skunk ordeal as the incident that began winning him over to Mr. Nak. "Yeah, that was pretty funny."

"Lawsuits are no laughing matter, Bo. The district could pay a hefty settlement."

Bo places his empty cup on the coffee table. "What's going on, you get elected to the school board or something?"

"No," Luke says, "but like any taxpayer, I'm interested in school business."

This doesn't feel right. "You've been 'hearing' a lot lately," Bo says. "Anything else I should know?"

"Actually there is one more thing, but I'd kind of decided to let it sit."

"Uh-huh, but now that the cat's out of the bag . . ."

Luke shakes his head. "It's not important. It's . . ."

"Come on, Dad. You know you're going to tell me."

"It's about one of your teachers. Something I thought you might want to be cautious of."

A new wave of uneasiness washes over Bo.

"It's one you like, the fellow who teaches Journalism. He's your swim coach, too, isn't he?"

This is a setup, Bo thinks, you *know* he's my swim coach. "What about him?"

"Just something I heard. Something I think you should be cautious—"

"What about him?"

"Well, I hear he's a bit strange, if you know what I mean." Luke raises his eyebrows and gives a limp wrist.

"What? Where did you hear that?"

"Does he have a wife? A girlfriend?"

"Hell, I don't know," Bo says. "Dad, Mr. Serbousek is not a homo."

"Now how would you know that?"

"I just know it, that's all. Who told you that?"

"That's not important. Just know this: It was a reliable source, as you journalistic types like to say."

Bo is once more amazed at how their conversations turn sour. "Well, it's not true."

Luke sits forward, deadly serious. "You be careful of him, son. Damn careful. You never know what those guys have in mind."

"Dad! Lion Serbousek is not a homosexual, okay?"

"First-name basis," Luke muses. Then, "You watch yourself, son."

"Jesus, Dad . . ."

"Why don't you run on home now? I'm sure your mom and your brother are holding up Christmas activities for you."

"Dad—"

"You go ahead. Run along. I'm fine here."

"I know you're fine. I just want to clear this . . . who told you that?"

"Go."

Nak intertwines his fingers over his knee and rocks slowly back on his desktop. "So, buckaroos, welcome back."

There are grunts.

"Everbody have a good vacation? Ready to get back into the tough stuff?"

More grunts.

"Anybody tear down the family Christmas tree?"

"Came close," Joey says.

Hudgie begins shaking his head continuously in slow motion. "No Christmas tree here, Mr. Nak. No Christmas tree. 'Sorry, Hudge. No Christmas tree for you. Can't have no Christmas tree, 'cause you're gettin' no Christmas. Wouldn't be right. No Christmas, no tree. Ya done messed up your Christmas, boy.'" He stares through Nak. "Couldn't tear it down, Mr. Nak. Wasn't there to tear. Not there to tear." Hudgie seems delighted with his primitive poetry. "Not there to tear," he says again. "Would've, though. Would've teared it to the ground."

Shuja watches uneasily, hoping he's not about to witness another Hudgie cave-in. He says, "Maybe nex' year, my man. You hold out for a tree nex' year, Hudge."

Hudgie looks at Shuja as though he's never seen him before. Shuja says, "Mr. Nak . . ."

"You all right, Hudge? You with us?" Mr. Nak asks.

Hudgie looks at his shoes and slowly nods his head.

"Good. Now let's git this show on the road. Who wants to start?"

Elvis, chin in palms, elbows resting on knees, slowly, tentatively, straightens up and raises his hand.

Nak says, "Still waitin' for orders to ride on out of here?"

"No, man," Elvis says back, uncharacteristically subdued. "I was just gonna let you in on Christmas at our house."

Nak says, "Shoot."

Elvis stares around the group, pausing at Bo to give a suspicious glare. Then, "My dad got a present from my sister. First time in twelve years."

Nak nods while the group waits. When Elvis doesn't offer more, Nak says, "What was it?"

Elvis's gaze drops to his knees, then back. "It was a bullet."

"Your sister shoot your daddy?" Shuja asks.

"No," Elvis says. "It was a present. Wrapped up and shit. My sister don't live with us. I mean, she's married, got kids."

Nak says, "Tell us about the present."

"Well, like I said, it was a bullet."

"And . . ."

Elvis glances again at the faces of the group members. "Look, you said we could talk about anything, right? Like, it don't have to be about some shit that pisses us off."

Nak says, "That's right," and the rest of the group falls even more silent. This is a different Elvis than the one any of them knows. Even Hudgie's attention is drawn.

"Rules the same?"

"What's gettin' under your saddle, Elvis?"

"Nobody talks outside of here. Shit that's said here, stays here?"

Nak nods, his eyes meeting Elvis's. "Yes." He turns his attention to the group as a whole. "I'll say it agin," he says. "Nothin' much gets me riled, I think you all know that. But if I hear any of you talkin' about what happens here to anyone who ain't here, you're gonna have a load o' me to deal with. Everbody okay with that?"

That's how he commands all that power, Bo thinks. He lays back until something's really important, then he comes on full blast.

Nak's request is met with quiet unanimity.

His gaze drifts back to Elvis. "That's good enough?"

"I guess," Elvis says. "Has to be. 'Cept I don't trust Brewster."

Bo's face instantly flushes.

"And why is that?" Nak asks.

"He ain't one of us. Look at him. Look at his clothes. Hell, look at his face. He ain't one of us."

Shelly's head snaps up, her look combative. "You haven't talked since you came here, Elvis. You don't get to decide who's one of us and who isn't."

"Maybe I do and maybe I don't," Elvis says calmly, "but no matter who decides, you are and Brewster ain't. Them fancy jock clothes don't fool me, sweetheart, you been through some shit. You ain't makin' all them muscles for looks."

"Keep talking, and I'll try them out on you," Shelly says.

Nak interrupts. "Whoa, whoa. You can head over to the OK Corral when we're done here. Meantime, let's get on with it. You ain't talkin' outsidea here, are you, Bo?"

"No."

"That's good enough for me. Go ahead, Elvis. Tell us about the bullet."

Elvis's eyes narrow at Bo. "I'm warnin' you, Brewster."

"He's good, Elvis. Tell us about the bullet."

"It was the one my old lady killed herself with. She was Dad's first wife. He's been through three more."

Dead silence.

"I didn't know your mother committed suicide, Elvis," Nak says after a moment. "I'm sorry to hear it."

Elvis shakes his head quickly. "No matter. Happened a long time ago, before we moved here. Four years."

Gazes fall to the floor as Elvis glances yet again around the room, with the exception of Hudgie's, which is wide-eyed frozen on Elvis's face. Elvis catches it, is seemingly unnerved, suddenly hesitant.

Nak reads his mind. "We're all in it now, Elvis. Go on ahead. Tell us about your mother. Tell us about the bullet."

"Came in a box," Elvis says finally. "All wrapped up nice in paper an' ribbons. There was a card. We was at the dinner table, me an' my little brother and sister an' my old man. He opened the box 'cause it didn't say who it was from; couldn'ta known what was in it. There was all this tissue paper an' cotton, an' right in the middle was this bullet, been spent. So Dad says, 'What the hell?' an' opens the card. His eyes like to pop out of his head while he's readin' it, then he looks over my head an' out the window—looks scared like I ain't never seen him—an' he reads it again. Then he jumps up an' runs to his room. Knocks a pan off the stove an' kicks over a lamp on his way. Gets on his coat an' he's gone."

Shuja says, "So how long he gone for? Mussa been one dyn-o-mite epistle."

"Never come back," Elvis says, and takes a deep breath. "My goddamn little sister an' brother start bawlin', an' I tell 'em to shut the hell up or I'll give them somethin' to bawl about, but that don't do no good, an' I run out the door to see where he's headed, but he's long gone. Pickup's still in the driveway."

Nak says, "You git your hands on the note?"

"Yeah, it was layin' right there on his bed." Elvis takes inventory of the faces again, and Nak gently urges him on.

"It said, 'This here's the bullet they took out of our momma's brain, Dad. I thought you should have it to put in the scrapbook I hope you're keepin' to show how bad you messed up this family. I'm tellin' what you did to me, Dad. I have to. It probably means you'll go to jail. It wasn't right.' "

Shelly scrutinizes Elvis's face, now staring into the floor in the middle of the circle. Softly she says, "You know what that means, don't you?"

"Yeah," he says without looking up. "It means my ol' man done my sister. Whaddaya think, I'm some kind of dumbshit?"

"No," Shelly says back evenly. "I just think it feels real bad, that's all. I know a thing or two about that."

Elvis flares. "Yeah, well, you don't know nothin' about me."

"I do now," she says.

Elvis stands and starts to bolt out of the room, but Nak's soft voice catches him midstride. "This ain't about Shelly," he says, "or any of the rest of us. No need to be runnin' off. Let's finish this. You told us for a reason. What was it?"

"I don't know," Elvis says, running his hand over his face in frustration. "I guess 'cause my brother an' sister are gettin' hungry an' I'm tired of stealin' shit to feed 'em, 'cause if I get caught, well . . ." Elvis appears desperate.

Nak nods.

"An' 'cause I'm feelin' like killin' my sister, but that's mostly 'cause I can't find my dad to kill him."

"You want to talk a little about your dad?" Nak asks.

"Nope. I'm done talkin'."

JANUARY 3

Dear Larry,

This saga is taking some *turns*. We might have to upgrade it to a "Knots Landing" spin-off. Maybe cable. Late night. Since it's supposed to be a book about my rise to the top of the triathletes' pyramid, I only wanted to include my training and what I think about during my training, but when I'm working out, my mind runs wild.

Do you find it strange to know about people's lives, Larry? I mean, it's got to affect you to talk to a 1950s Miss America after you know her dad molested her, right? It changes things. Being in Mr. Nak's group shows you what's below the surface of people's lives. When you're just trying to live your life, trying to get by, you tend to oversimplify things. You look at a guy like Elvis, and he's just another badass making all us regular folks' lives a little more risky, and Hudgie's a loon and Shelly is there to make you ache below the belt, and Mr. S is there to help you, and I'm just breathing people's air. But when you look below the surface, something else is true.

If I ever do really mail any of this to you, I'll have to white a lot of it out, especially this next part because it's confidential and the guy it's about already thinks I'm a major snitch, but writing it down might help me understand it. Today Elvis told us his older sister accused his dad of being a child molester. She sent him the bullet their mother killed herself with when she found out, as a little Christmas reminder that he drove her to it. Shuja was squirming like he was ten seconds from blast-off, and nearly everyone else tried to disappear to keep from looking at Elvis or have his story touch them in any way. But Hudgie was calmer than I've ever seen him. I don't know, Larry; *something* about the two of them was the same. It was like Hudge knew something, and Elvis knew he knew it. All way below the surface.

And it started me thinking about my own dad. On Christmas Eve, we talked about some things we disagree about, and it was the first time I've ever seen my father maybe doubt himself a little. He didn't admit it—we'll both be old guys when that happens—but I saw a tear, and it made me hope for a truce, or at least a cease-fire. Naturally, the second I had the thought, he started baiting me with some trash about Mr. S that was really ridiculous, and it all went south. To tell the truth, I think I helped sabotage it because I was afraid of the complications it might bring between him and me—you know, remind me how much I want to love him—when I'm trying my best to hold my own.

Then hearing Elvis today made me think I didn't have a lot to bitch about, but when I said that to Mr. Nak after group, he said, "Don't get to thinkin' just because some other guy's sinkin' in horse manure, the stuff up around your neck is chocolate puddin'. A wound is a wound, young Brewster. Remember that. Don't diminish the pain of your own just because you see some other gut-shot cowboy bleedin' to death." Then he said, "You ain't signed up for much longer. I'd get some stuff off my chest if I was you."

Be ready, Lar. If I tell them, I tell you.

Your eyes and ears in the Northwest,

The Brewmeister

"Stotan: a cross between a Stoic and a Spartan," Bo says, a Cheshire grin spreading across his face. "Coined by an Australian track coach named Perciville Cerruti about thirty or so years ago, in describing Herb Elliot, world record holder in the mile run."

"Not bad," Lion says, glancing up at Bo from his desk. "That didn't take you long."

"That's not all," Bo says back. "More recently—mid-eighties, in fact—the term was used to describe the last swimming team at Robert Frost High School in the great and scenic city of Spokane, Washington."

"I'm impressed. I'd call that pretty thorough investigative reporting."

"I'd call it *very* thorough," Bo says. "The first part came from the microfiche in the library and the second part from the office."

"The school office?"

"You forget who the vice-principal at Frost was back then?"

The light of realization passes over Lion's face. "Aha, the honorable Dr. Stevens."

"Yes, indeed," Bo says. "And once she started spilling her guts, it was nearly impossible to shut the interview down. Did you really paint socks on your legs so they'd let you into your prom?"

Lion smiles. "And a fine pair they were. A bit hairy, but they fit like they were custom-made."

"And did the toilet in your apartment really have a seat belt?"

"Kept my friends from blasting off," Lion says in affirmation.

"You were weird."

"Perhaps lacking maturity in some key areas."

"I think I might scrap the American Gladiators piece and do a little exposé," Bo says. "Say, something in an unauthorized biographical sketch."

Lion reaches into his shirt pocket, extracting a red pen. "Know what this is?"

"You're about to tell me."

"It is the sword of censorship, young man, the sword of censorship. Stick to your star-crossed Gladiator."

"So tell me about the modern-day Stotans."

Lion sits back. "Strictly off the record," he says, staring at the ceiling. "We had this amazing coach, a lot like Mr. Nak, really. He was a Korean guy named Max Il-Song. Grew up in Montana. He read the *Sports Illustrated* article you found on the microfiche and became so enthralled with Herb Elliot's work ethic that he designated the first week of Christmas vacation of our senior year as Stotan Week. There were only four of us on the team, and we all moved into my apartment, which, besides having a seat belt on the toilet, had no heat or light and no furniture. We put sleeping bags on bare mattresses and hunkered down for the week, which turned out to be your basic juggernaut of pain."

Lion takes a deep breath, reveling in the memory. "From eight in the morning until noon, for five days, we worked out without one second's rest. The intervals between repeats were filled with push-ups, sit-ups, chin-ups on the high board, bear walk around the pool. And there were repeated trips to the Torture Lane any time Max thought we were letting up."

Bo is absorbed. "The Torture Lane?"

"Twenty-five-yard sprint, ten push-ups, twenty-five-yard sprint, ten push-ups, twenty-five-yard sprint, ten push-ups, until *he* got tired. I don't know how we did it."

"How *did* you do it?"

"Together," Lion said. "We did it together. I met two of those guys at our five-year reunion—the other one had died—and we stayed up all night talking about how none of us could have done it alone, but no one could have quit as long as the others hung in."

"God," Bo says. "A four-hour workout with no rest?"

"Not one second," Lion says back. "Not one second." He gazes into the fluorescent lights in the ceiling. "Max played us like a symphony. Wrung out every last harmonic chord. God, I loved those guys."

"One of them died?"

Lion nods. "Yeah. Jeff Hawkins. Big, strong redhead. Toughest guy I ever knew. Got some poison in his blood cells and just shriveled up and went away."

Bo feels suddenly uneasy with this intimate glimpse into his teacher's life, but intrigued. "Was he your friend?"

"Oh, yeah," Lion says. "He was my friend."

A silence falls between them as other students file into the room. "God," Bo says finally, "I hope that never happens to me."

"I hope so, too."

"So," Bo says as the bell rings signaling the beginning of class, "you said I should go at the Yukon Jack's piece from a Stotan point of view. How am I going to do that? I train alone, except for swimming with you guys, and I don't think there are many CFU swimmers willing to sign a Stotan pact with me. Hell, Wyrack would kill them."

"I can't tell you where to find them," Lion says, "but take a piece of advice from a pro. Choose your fellow Stotans carefully."

"I don't think you should always train with these dogs," Shelly says, watching Bo slip a harness over the broad head of Buck, an eighty-five-pound red male husky, in the early morning five-degree temperature.

"Why not?" Bo snaps a connecting chain to the harness of the equally eager Samantha, a forty-five-pound silver female, then stuffs his hands into his mittens.

"Because they can't run in Yukon Jack's. These guys are responsible for most of your speed the first three or four miles. All you do is hold on and move your legs."

"If it's an inferior workout, how come I can't breathe after the first hundred yards? Besides, I got no choice. If I don't run them every day, they'll attack and eat me. I'll just add miles."

"I have a better idea."

"Why am I not surprised?"

"Because you're beginning to wise up."

Bo's eyebrows rise. "So what's your idea?"

"A sled."

Bo snorts. *"There's* a better idea. If a little dog power diminishes the effect of your training, why not wipe out your workouts altogether and ride?"

Shelly smiles. *"I* ride, Brainiac. You run along beside."

Bo thinks a minute. "I don't know. These guys have never actually pulled a sled. They've only pulled me."

"Yeah, but they're sled dogs. Believe me, Brew, they'll catch on. And I'll be the Susan Butcher of the lower forty-eight."

"Who's Susan Butcher?"

"The next best thing to an Alaskan Gladiator. She used to win the Iditarod on a fairly regular basis—against scores of macho numbnuts just like Ian Wyrack."

"Would you mind telling me something?" Bo scrutinizes Shelly across the booth at Doc's.

She shrugs. "Take a chance."

"What did you mean the other day in Mr. Nak's group when you told Elvis you knew what he was talking about?"

"Child molestation?" she says. "You can say it, Brew."

"Yeah, that."

"Because I have an uncle who's gifted in that area."

"Really? Did he—I mean, did you—"

"Get molested? Nope. But my sister did, and so did two of my cousins." Shelly speaks with no hint of emotion. "I told. Almost got me thrown out of the house. It did get me beat up. This was clear back in grade school."

"Who beat you up?"

"Who always beat me up? My dad. My sister chickened out

after I told and wouldn't back me up, and my cousins called me a liar and a bitch. Dad couldn't figure out why I would say such things, so he slapped hell out of me to make me stop. Said I was making the family look bad."

"God, what did you do?"

"I covered my head, what would you do? But he was *really* mad, and he got in a shot that cracked my eye socket. My sister wouldn't protect herself, but she'd sure protect me, so she got on the phone and called Child Protection Services." Shelly laughs, void of delight. "Man, those guys were there in fifteen minutes with the cops, and they put my dad away for the weekend and got my uncle for 'communication with a minor.' Isn't that amazing? They called what he did to her 'communication.' He didn't do much jail time, but he disappeared when he got out, and no one in the family's seen him since—which probably means some girl none of us knows is getting it as we speak."

Bo watches her face, looking for signs of the war she just described. "You tell it like you're talking about a family reunion or something."

"Want me to burst into tears? Or tear this booth out of the floor?"

Bo chuckles. "No, I guess not. These people will think I did something." He hesitates, formulating a question he has danced around since he's known her. "Can I ask you something?"

"Like when are we going to have sex?"

Bo's chin drops as if he's placed a five-pound pinch of BBs between his lower lip and gum. "No! I mean that's not what I was going to ask. I mean, I just wanted to know . . ." He pauses. "When *are* we going to have sex?"

JANUARY 8

Dear Larry,

I think it's about time you did a show on safe sex. You probably have, but advertising has more clout when you're in the market for the product. Let me clarify my request. I'm not requesting a show on creative uses of the condom; my PE teacher has already demanded that we each have one welded to the appropriate appendage as we step out of the shower each morning. I'm talking about a show that will demonstrate how to be safe if you go to bed with someone who can pin you three falls out of three.

Only kidding, Lar. Shelly talked about having sex today when we were in Doc's, and it threw me off. We've only been making out a little while, and my fantasies—not to mention my skills—aren't finely honed enough to step up into the majors. Actually, she brought it up to keep from talking about a subject she wanted to avoid, and it worked for a while, but I prevailed.

She's *so* fine, Larry. At first I think her muscles might have put me off a bit, but her skin is soft as suede and kind of naturally tan, and though she's not movie-star gorgeous, she's *maximum* sexy. And see, that's part of the problem, because I can't think about getting serious without thinking about that part, but I also can't think about getting serious without wanting to know all I can about her, because I think that's how my parents got into trouble, by not knowing each other.

Remember, I met her in Anger Management, which has to be, on the whole, a really bad dating service; and after all this time I still don't know exactly why she's there. And unless you're a misunderstood righteous dude such as myself, you have to commit some true ugliness to be sent there. So I finally cut through all the bullshit and asked. I said, "So how did you get into the Nak Pack?"

"I asked him if I could."

"You mean you're not sentenced to it?"

She shook her head.

"I don't get it."

"My whole life is full of secrets," she said. "Secrets are the very worst thing you can have in your life, Bo, and that's all there is in mine. My family views the truth like it's cholera, and they stomp it out. My dad broke my eye socket because he would rather beat me up than let the truth out, or have his family look bad." Then she said, "You know why I took a liking to you right off?" and I said, "Biceps? Quads?"

She said, "Yeah, right. No, it was because of Redmond."

I hesitated a long second before saying, "I do not fancy the idea of owing Mr. When the Going Gets Tough for the luckiest break of my life. *Please* tell me this has twisted meaning."

She said, "This has twisted meaning. You sure you want to hear it?"

I was sure.

"Besides all the secrecy in my family, my parents are just plain nuts. They're nuts and they're mean. Most of the time I think they adopted me because they needed one kid to hate. They've always said they love me as much as my brother and sisters, who are all biological, but it's a lie. I never even got the same allowance as they did."

"They gave you less allowance? That's *cold*."

"That's not even the bad part. I was the only jock of the bunch, and in all my years in grade school and junior high they never went to one game, and I played three sports. When I was eight, if I couldn't find a ride to summer soccer, I walked three miles. Dad said it would help me get in shape."

"So how does this make Redmond responsible for awakening you to the social and sexual potency of Beauregard Brewster?"

"*That* would be a rude awakening. Be patient. Mom said I hated her from the beginning, and Dad said he knew I was a troublemaker from day one. As far back as I can—"

I said, "Wait. Your mother thought you hated her and your dad said you were a troublemaker the day they got you?"

She nodded. "That's what they said. They still say it."

"I thought my dad was rough."

"They'll tell you it was in my genes. Mom said my real mother was a drug addict and a prostitute, that I'd probably turn out the same." Shelly gazed over my head and out the window. "You can't know how much that scared me. I didn't even know what a drug addict was, or a prostitute, either, but I knew they were bad and I really believed I could make my parents love me if I could just be good enough to prove I wouldn't turn out like my real mom. I watched enough TV to know if you were good at sports you'd never be a drug addict or a prostitute."

I still wanted to know what this had to do with Redmond or her liking me.

"In seventh grade I heard about this agency that will search for your real parents, and by then I was starting to give up on pleasing my mom and dad, and I was so miserable I would rather have lived with a prostitute and a drug addict than with them, so I got a paper route, because the people who did the search charged two hundred and fifty dollars."

"That's a lot of newspapers."

"It is a *lot* of newspapers, but I made the money and they started the process. It only took them two weeks to tell me she'd been a college student right here at CFU on a partial track scholarship. They couldn't give me her name until they tracked her down and got her permission, but they said she gave me up because she wasn't ready to start a family yet. They also told me that even though my mother never actually met her, she had that information." '

I said, "So how pissed were you?"

Shelly leaned forward on her elbows, Lar, clenching her teeth so hard I thought her jaw muscle would pop out the side of her face. "I got home from that meeting and went to my room and got my baseball bat and stormed into the kitchen and leveled it."

"What do you mean, leveled it?"

"I broke out the windows, ripped three cupboard doors off their hinges, stacked all the dishes I could find on the floor and dropped the microwave on them."

"Oh," I said. "You mean you *leveled* it."

She ignored me. "Mom tried to call Dad, but I tore the telephone cord out of the wall. Then I ran into the living room and fired a vase through the picture tube of our twenty-seven-inch TV, all the time screaming that my mother was a bitch and a drug addict and a goddamn liar!"

She was sweating as she told me, Lar, like *dripping*.

I asked what they did to her.

She said, "Foster care. Mom made it across the street and called my dad and the cops. I was lucky the cops got there first, because Dad would have beaten me bloody. I went to the Crisis Residential Center for a few days, and since I wouldn't quit threatening to light my parents' house on fire, they found me a placement."

"God, what was that like?"

She shrugged. "Actually, it could have been okay. They were probably nice people, but I was so angry I just hid out in my room. They were kind of afraid of me, I think, and I started getting in trouble at school, skipping classes, smoking dope, doing all the things my mother had said were in my genes."

I wanted to ask if she did the other part, Lar, but I tell you, I'm getting smart. This girl could take me *out*.

"I was kicked out of three junior high schools and five foster homes before the school year was over. By that time there was no drug I wouldn't try and nobody's ass I wouldn't kick." She sighed and her shoulders slumped, and I figured now was the time.

I said, "So how does Redmond fit into this?"

Her eyes flared. "I spent the rest of junior high in residential treatment at Good Shepherd. I was so much trouble at first, they stuck me in isolation for days on end to break me, but I'd be out a day or two and some girl would look cross-eyed at me and I'd take her out, and back I'd go to this locked room with nothing but a bed. They'd make me wait to go to the bathroom until I thought I'd explode."

I flinched, and she said, "I know, you want to know about Redmond."

I said, "I can wait. This is a good story."

"It's a shitty story," she said back, "but it's true. I was still at Good Shep when I got out of junior high, and I was thrown out of two high schools in Spokane and one in the valley. I guess I finally started wearing down because I finally got tired of being in trouble all the time and having everyone hate me or be scared of me or both, and I was sick of being *alone*. I had also let my body go completely to hell. I weighed as much as a hundred-sixty pounds and as little as one-oh-three.

"So I made a plan. For the next six months I was a model citizen. My room was immaculate, I ran errands for the other girls, cleaned the premises without being asked. I worked out every day, even though I was being schooled on the grounds and couldn't play on any more teams because they didn't want me trashing any more schools. Six months. Bring me an ass and I'd kiss it.

"Then in September of what should have been my sophomore year, I got myself sprung from Good Shep and placed with a family here in Clark Fork. Good people, and far enough away from anyone who knew my history that I might have a chance."

I guessed. "This is where Redmond comes in."

"This is where Redmond comes in. He was coaching girls' basketball and I turned out. I'd been playing basketball since I was six years old—mostly with boys in my neighborhood. I was most valuable player two years in a row in age group, on a team that almost went to *Nationals*, Brew. This was a good team and I was one of the best players on it. I *loved* basketball."

I leaned back in my seat and slowly shook my head. It could be no other way. "Redmond cut you."

Shelly looked off to the side as tears welled in her eyes.

"Why?"

She was silent a moment more, gathering herself. Shelly doesn't like to let even me see the hurt side of her. "The night before cut day, I didn't sleep a second. I wasn't worried about being cut, but I wanted to make varsity. I'd given it everything I had: ran every drill full speed, dived for balls, shot jumpers until my arms almost fell off. I wouldn't leave the gym until I'd dropped ten free throws in a row."

"So how the hell did he cut you?"

Shelly pounded her fist into her palm so hard I thought she broke something, Lar, and then thumped her chest. "Twice in practice I almost blew up. Once a girl undercut me and I came up with my fists cocked. She walked away, and I followed, yelling 'Hey!' but she kept walking. I caught myself that time and apologized, but Redmond saw. The other time a girl fell on my knee. I thought I was injured and came up swinging. My rage would just appear like that. Redmond jumped between us and sent me to the lockers. I apologized again, but I was still worried he'd put me on JV for it."

"Did he?"

Shelly grimaced. "Nope. You played football, so you know about cut day. They posted two sheets—one for varsity and one for JV—at noon in student lunch. The whole team crowded around as they were being posted. I scanned the varsity list and didn't see my name, but I wasn't as disappointed as I thought I'd be, because by then I'd prepared myself by saying if it happened, I'd work so hard and play so well they'd have to move me up in midseason, or at least by tournament time. But then I scanned the JV list, and my name wasn't there, either. I started laughing, because I knew I'd gone over the varsity list so fast I'd missed it. But when I looked again, my name wasn't there. It wasn't anywhere."

I said, "Oh, God. What—"

"I was the only kid cut. There was a foreign exchange

student from Sweden who had never touched a basketball in her life, Brew, and she made JV."

"What did you do?"

"All of a sudden I felt naked. I knew everyone was looking at me, and I was completely stripped. Panic was choking me, so I smiled and started to walk away. I just needed to get to the door, get outside. One of the girls grabbed my arm. She said it had to be a mistake and she would go talk to Redmond with me right that minute, but by then I was claustrophobic. I couldn't breathe and I just needed to get out, so I ran."

"But it wasn't a mistake, was it? Redmond meant to cut you."

"No mistake," she said. "But this story gets better. I went home and snagged my foster mother's car and headed for the freeway at about a hundred miles an hour. It sounds suicidal, I know, but I really wanted to hit something, make somebody hurt. Luckily I wasn't much of a driver, and I skidded into the highway divider and flipped a couple of times. Totaled the car, but I didn't have a scratch."

"Jeez, Shelly, you're lucky to be alive."

"I guess that depends on your definition of lucky."

"Okay," I said. "I'm lucky you're alive. Did you find out why Redmond did it?"

"Sure did. My foster family gave me the boot in about the same amount of time it took the tow truck to get to the car. They said they were sorry, but they couldn't stand it if a kid got killed in their care. When my child protection caseworker came out to get me, I told him why I did it, and he went with me to confront Redmond."

"I'll bet that was fun."

"Actually, it was, kind of. My caseworker, Jim Avery, was this great big guy—bigger than Redmond—and an ex-Golden Gloves boxer. I thought he was going to spar a couple of rounds with Redmond, which would have made it all worth it."

I dream of the day, Lar. I dream of the day.

"Well, at first Jim was very polite, and he explained my situation to Redmond and asked if there was a way he would reconsider letting me play. Redmond said that after he saw how willing I was to mix it up, he had requested my records and decided he couldn't afford to have someone poisoning the team's morale, that it wasn't fair to the other girls. Jim stayed polite long enough to get Redmond to admit that I had the talent to play, then he threatened to sue the school on behalf of the state of Washington and on behalf of me."

This is the kind of shit I like, Lar.

"Redmond said go right ahead, that the conversation was off the record. He said certain kids simply weren't right for high-school athletics, no matter what their talent—particularly those who had used up their chances."

Redmond's sensitivity and tolerance know no bounds, Lar. I can't believe I'm the only one in Nak's Pack for calling him an asshole. We ought to take out a class-action billboard.

So Shelly kind of smiled and said, "I was just getting ready to use the F-word in reference to Redmond when Jim beat me to it. He told Redmond he had no business within five hundred miles of a kid and that he would register a formal complaint with the Clark Fork school board, and if that didn't work he'd sue him for malpractice. He also said Redmond better never give him the slightest reason to kick his ass out in the real world, because he would do it with gusto and in front of as many people as possible."

Whooo! Hey, Lar, I wanna meet this Jim guy.

Shelly said, "I think that saved me. I was devastated at losing basketball, but it was the first time an adult ever stood up for me. Jim and I went out for coffee to try to figure out my future. We decided it probably wouldn't be much fun for me to play for Redmond, what with this much sewage under the bridge. The bigger problem was that he was out of foster placements for me, so my choices were to go home or back to Good Shep.

"My dad was tired of paying the state for my room and board all over town, so he agreed to let me move into this little guest house out back and keep his goddamn hands off me and my mother off my back as much as he could. CPS sent me home mostly because everybody was just so worn down. I stayed in school out here because it was the only place I'd ever had any success."

"I take it the state never tried to bring the house down on Redmond." I knew the answer, because Redmond is still up to his SOS.

"Naw," she said. "If Dr. Stevens had been here then, we would have gone for it, but Mr. Cox was just a better-dressed form of Redmond and I didn't need those guys thinking of ways to make me mad enough to get kicked out. Jim signed me up for some martial-arts classes up at CFU and got me the phony ID so I could use the weight room. Actually it was Jim who came up with the idea of me being a Gladiator. That guy walked out to the edge for me. I owe him big."

I said I'd like to meet him someday.

"He's gone. They kicked him upstairs to Olympia. But I'll never forget him." She put her hand over mine. "So you see, Brew, Elvis was right. I am one of them, and you aren't."

I smiled and said I'd work harder.

"Anyway, it's too late to make a long story short, but I told Mr. Nak about the kitchen and the TV, and about Redmond. I told him my feelings about my parents haven't changed that much, so it could probably happen again."

"What'd he say?"

"He said, 'Not only can you join my git-together, little lady, you can be our poster girl. I ain't never met anyone your size done in a whole kitchen, then had enough left to do in a giant television. I'm impressed.'" She said it in perfect Nakatanese.

Then she said, "Does that scare you off?" and I said it didn't. That was only partially true, because though it didn't scare me *off*, it sure made me jumpy.

I said, "What happens if I inadvertently tell a little lie?" and she said she would probably inadvertently kick my ass, so I told her I thought the new blouse she was wearing was ugly even though I'd said I liked it earlier.

She laughed and said, "Truth is, Brew, I'm never going to hit anybody I care about. That's the hell of my family— and it stops here."

I don't know, Lar. I went home after I talked to Shelly and wondered how she could be this neat and have lived through the nightmare she described. And I thought about how guys like Redmond get their power. Where does it come from and how do you fight it? I'll bet Mr. S has some ideas, and for sure Mr. Nak would. Tell you what, I don't think I'll be leaving Nak's Pack anytime soon.

One thing I'd like to achieve in my quest for Ironmanliness is some wisdom about the nature of justice. Any ideas, Lar?

> Ever your loyal fan,
>
> The Brewder

"God, sometimes I just hate my dad," Bo says. He sits in Gatto's across the booth from Lionel Serbousek, waiting for their pepperoni-and-sausage pizza. They have come to organize training strategies for Yukon Jack's.

"I'd be careful of that if I were you," Lion says.

"You wouldn't if you knew my dad."

"I don't know your dad," Lion says, "but I knew mine."

Bo is instantly embarrassed. Everyone knows Mr. S was orphaned at fourteen, when his family was killed in a freak boating accident across the state line on Lake Coeur d'Alene. Only Lion survived. "Oh, God, man, I'm sorry. I didn't mean . . ."

Lion lifts his hand in protest. "Don't worry about it. I said it because my dad was a lot like yours. He liked control—needed it—and he was hard to deal with when he felt he was losing it."

"They sound like brothers."

"They do, don't they?"

"So what did you do about it?"

"Argued a lot," Lion says. "Tried to piss him off as much as possible." He hesitates as their pizza number is called over the intercom, and Bo rises to retrieve it.

"We were scrapping a bit that day on the boat," he says when Bo returns. "Arguing about responsibility and fishing."

"You were arguing about fishing?"

"Fishing demanded all the attributes my father believed led to an exemplary life," Lion says. "It required intelligence and patience, and though there were no guarantees, one could certainly stack the deck in his favor by doing it right." Lion has considered his story a thousand times, told it few. He believes

Bo should hear it. "We'd been fishing from the boat near shore, under an overhang of bushes. I was beat from a night of screwing around with my friends and didn't even want to be there. My little brother and Mom were up front, as far as they could get from Dad's relentless instructions. The bait was up with them and I was too lazy to get it, so I baited my hook with berries from a bush hanging out over the boat."

"You were fishing with berries?" Bo laughs. "I don't fish and even I know—"

"Yeah, well," Lion interrupts, "so did Dad. And don't think he didn't let me in on it. You know how your father palms the back of his neck when he's getting close to the edge? Well, my dad would shake his head in this certain way. He'd grimace and look at the ground and then shake his head real slow." Lion imitates memory. "Whenever I got on a self-improvement kick, I'd promise myself to reduce the number of times per day Dad did that."

Bo thinks of his own dad. "It didn't work, did it? You didn't reduce that number one bit."

"Not one bit," Lion says with a smile. He sips his beer and places a slice of pizza on his plate. "His head shook in classic fashion while he watched me reel in those berries; fishing was just too important to my dad to be trivialized. He had to give me the long version of his responsibility speech before he'd even start the engine to head for deeper water. I called it his You Got to *Think* speech."

Bo nods. "The Someday When You're My Age speech."

"I'm sure that's it."

Bo feels oddly relieved that someone else knows this.

"But you know something?" Lion says. "That speech isn't completely wrong; it's just badly delivered—and the timing's off. The truth is, I did have to think; I did have to consider my actions more carefully. Not about fishing, necessarily, but about other things. And the world does look different when that someday comes and you're older. It doesn't necessarily look the way your dad thinks it will, but it's certainly different. I think that speech could have helped if it had been given more gently—hadn't had such weight attached."

Bo takes a long drink of ice water, having given up on sugary pops in the name of training, and half a slice of pizza disappears into his mouth. "I don't know, Mr. S. You should hear my old man."

"I know, Bo, believe me I know. I'm just saying it doesn't help to discard the good news with the bad." He scoots his chair back and intertwines his fingers behind his thick neck, staring at the ceiling. "I thought I had time. I thought I had all of time. Now not a day goes by that I don't want to talk with my dad, learn more of where I come from. I know we'd still fight, and there are issues we'd never agree on, but I just wasn't ready for it to be over."

Lion leans forward on his elbows. "It was killer hot out there that day on the lake, easily over a hundred degrees. Neal Anderson, this kid I swam with in age group, was over at his parents' summer cabin drinking beer with some of his buddies. He was fourteen, just like me. His mom and dad didn't even know he was there—thought he'd gone to a matinee back in Spokane to get out of the heat. After a couple of six-packs they got to yukkin' it up and decided to take a quick spin on the skis.

"I saw 'em coming, even thought I recognized the boat, a sleek yellow Sunrunner, one of the fastest ski boats on the lake. When I dream about it now, I see it as a thing of awful beauty, skipping like a bullet over the sun stars dancing on the glassy surface."

Bo sits fascinated, afraid to hear the rest.

"I jumped," Lion says, and shakes his head, teary-eyed. "I yelled and when they didn't hear me, I jumped." He sits back. "You know, Bo, there is a feeling, in that instant following some life-changing tragedy, that you can actually step back over that sliver of time and stop the horror from coming. But that feeling is a lie, because in the tiniest microminisecond after any event occurs, it is as safe in history as Julius Caesar. Data in the universal computer is backed up *as it happens*. That's probably a good thing for me, too, because given a chance to think, I'd have stayed in the boat.''

Bo stares at the edge of the table, speechless.

''*In the water* I was already sorry for the bad things I'd done, all I hadn't said, and most of what I had. After all our disagreements—no, fights—after all our fights, I just wanted my dad to approve of me.''

''God, Mr. S . . .''

''I'm not saying you should torment yourself about people you love dying tomorrow, but I think it's smart to keep up to speed with those you consider important.''

Bo muches pizza, considering. ''You're right, Mr. S. I know you are, and there are times when I ache to please my dad, but you should hear him sometimes. I mean, he'll make up stories about people just to make his point. Hell, you should hear what he said about you.''

''Everyone has their ugliness,'' Lion says. ''That's not what I'm talking about. I'm talking about relationship. I'm talking about looking past the current war to find out what you are to each other.'' He pauses and shakes his head. ''It isn't simple, Bo. It should be, but it isn't. It's not about good guys and bad guys, or right and wrong. It's something way more basic than those things. It's about connection. I sit back and watch you now, and know that part of your struggle is developmental— that as an adolescent, you need to separate from your dad to establish who you are. I'm frustrated because I want *you* to learn from *my* experience, and I know that's not going to happen. But it is developmental, Bo. It's a time of life, a time of life that will change. I can only hope that you and your dad stay intact long enough to see it for what it is. I guess I'm just saying don't burn all your bridges.'' He pauses, lost in the flurry of his words. Then, ''What did he say about me?''

''Never mind, it—''

''You don't have to say it if you don't want to, Bo, but I'm a big boy. I can take it.''

Bo shifts nervously. "Well, we were fighting about Red-mond, you know, about good guys and bad guys, and he said . . ." He pauses. "It was nothing."

"Say it."

"Well, he said you were . . . like . . . homo; you know, *gay*."

A faint smile crosses Lion's lips, and he glances at the pizza.

"I mean, I didn't believe him. Shit, I mean, I don't know why . . ."

Lion remains silent as Bo is swept with a wave of realization. "Oh, God. Oh, no. Shit, Mr. S."

"What?"

"Are you?"

"Yes."

JANUARY 24

Dear Larry,

Had a great workout last night, Lar. Got home from pizza with Mr. S about seven-thirty, hitched up the dogs one at a time, and ran 'em five miles apiece. Then I went over to CFU and swam the last forty-five minutes of open lap swim and worked out on the StairMaster for thirty minutes. Then I lifted weights.

I know I'm talking to the wrong talk-show dude if I've got a beef about this, Lar, but I don't even know how to spell Lim-baa. My life is getting flat weird. This shit is strictly Geraldo.

Mr. S is a homo. I mean, he's gay. And that's not just some name a guy calls somebody to get his goat. He sleeps with a *man*. I mean, he doesn't sleep with him, necessarily; he has *sex* with him.

I'm sitting there in the pizza place with him last night trying to tell him what a peckerhead my dad can be, how he makes up stories about people he doesn't like, and I tell Mr. S Dad said he had a limp wrist. To which I expect Mr. S to laugh and say "sticks and stones" or something, but he just looks at me and I get all tongue-tied, just like

I'm pen-tied writing this to you, and he tells me it's no lie.

Well, I stuff down half a pizza about as fast as a guy can eat without a couple of Heimlich adjustments, and tell him I got a load of homework and I'll see him later. He says, "Instead of running off and turning your imagination into a three-ring circus, why don't you stay and talk about this?"

Like the dumb shit I truly am, I say, "Talk about what?"

Mr. S laughs and says, "Oh, I don't know, whatever pops into your head." Then he says, "About me being gay."

So after I try about fifteen false starts, he says, "Why don't you just ask me what you want to know?" and I come up with, "So are you coming out of the closet or what? How come you told me?"

He says, "There's no closet, Bo. I told you because you asked. I'm not an activist—my sexual preference is only a part of who I am. It's just that after my family was killed, I swore I would never again lie about anything important to any*one* important."

"You mean everyone knows? Does your swimming team know?"

"They've never asked," he said. "You're the first in quite a while, actually. It doesn't come up much."

This felt so crazy I had to push, Lar. I said, "So what if they knew? I mean, what do you think they'd do?"

"Whatever they had to," he said. "Bo, I didn't choose to be attracted to men, that's just the way it is. I chose to deal with it. Anyone who has a problem with that will have to do the same."

I knew he meant me, Lar, and I've heard you say something pretty close to that on your show, but I ignored it. "So how do you think my dad knew?"

"Your dad wouldn't know me if he walked through that door right now. I would guess Redmond said something."

"Jesus, Redmond knows?"

"He doesn't know, but he's guessed. He knows I have a male roommate, and he met Jack at a faculty Christmas party a couple of years ago. Keith doesn't like me any better than he likes you, so I would guess he has a gala time with it in my absence."

Now I hate to say it, Lar, because it sounds just like the guys who call you, and I know your bigot-basher nose must be twitching like a geiger counter at Los Alamos, waiting for me to write the comment that lets you know what kind of narrow-minded, hateful scum I am, but I don't think I'm a bigot. Hey, I've been in Mr. Nak's group awhile now, hearing people tell the most bizarre stories as if they're giving the weather report, and I'm even starting to like that style. I mean, Elvis tells us his dad got the bullet his mom committed suicide with for a Christmas present and that his sister is going to charge his dad with child molestation; Shelly talks about being beaten by her dad and double-crossed by Redmond; Hudgie doesn't really tell us anything, but he plays out the horrors of his life like they were a cereal commercial. But Mr. S dropped a *bomb* and there's just no other way to say it, and I don't think anyone—bigoted or not—should be expected to receive it over a pizza and go on as if the world hadn't just tilted on its axis.

What am I going to tell my dad? He'll say if I could be tricked about *that*, what else am I being tricked about? Then he'll tell me again how careful I should be. I mean, I don't *think* there's any danger, because I certainly have never felt anything like, you know, sexual, coming from Mr. S, but I can't help wondering if it means anything about me that he likes me. I stood up for Mr. S against my dad, and now I'll eat shit. And I'll tell you what, I don't know how I'm going to face Mr. S the next time I see him. I can't tell anybody because I don't want to get a bunch of rumors started, so I guess I'll have to figure it out for myself. This whole thing pisses me off. Why can't Mr. S just be normal? I need a normal guy to go up against guys like Redmond and my dad. Some Stotan, huh?

Gotta go, Lar. None of this is helping me focus on my training.

Sincerely drowning,

Bo Blub-Blub

CHAPTER 10

Dear Larry,

Here's a true story you can use on the air some time for filler. My little brother, Jordan, has always thought Martin Luther King, Jr., wrote the "I Have a Dream" speech specifically for him, because they have the same birthday, and from Jordan's first, he'd toddle into the living room to the strains of King's passionate voice as presented on the "Today" show.

From the time Jordan could walk, at about ten months, both my folks had a terrible time getting him down for a nap. Mom gave up trying, so by the time he was one and a half he spent naptime at our house on his bed playing with his toys or babbling or screaming. Mom said there was no reason for him to sleep if he didn't want to, but Dad had this idea that a nap was about the most important thing a kid could learn to take, so when Jordan stayed at his house, Dad put him down right after lunch to take the same goddamn nap Dad always took, the one I woke him up from when I slammed the door.

The freedom he enjoyed at our place wasn't easily relinquished at Dad's, and keeping him down for any length of time became a tougher and tougher challenge. And this kid did it right, Lar. He was noncompliant from day one, and he didn't scare. Dad couldn't admit his nap theory was full of holes, especially to my mother, but to save face and his blood pressure, he decided he had read somewhere that a kid needed forced daytime sleep only until his third birthday and he would back off immediately after that event, but not one day before. Mom knew he'd never read any such thing unless it was in a pre-Hitler German child-care manual, but it was almost Christmas when he said it, and she figured it wouldn't hurt Jordan to put up with this silliness for just another month. She kept telling Jordan it was like what the monkey said when they cut off his tail: "It won't be long now."

Jordan didn't get the pun, of course, but he got pretty excited about his third birthday, and not only because both my parents spent the equivalent of Ross Perot's tax refund on gifts for his spoiled butt. He was about to become nap-free. On the afternoon of that magnificent day, I pedaled him over to Dad's, where he bounded into the living room, onto the couch, spread his arms, and crowed, "Three at last! Three at last! Thank God Almighty, I'm three at last!"

Okay, I admit it, Lar. I coached him every day for three weeks leading up to his performance, but he pulled it off without a hitch. Much as I'd like to end his life in a slow and torturous way, I love that he's such a tenacious little hothead that he takes on Lucas Brewster in ways I never dreamed possible. The last time I plucked him out of his room at Dad's, he was sticking pins in a voodoo doll one of his buddies gave him at school and laughing like a maniac. He said, "*There's* one in your colon. Take that in your testes." Jeez, the kid is in *kindergarten,* and here he is sending psychic penetrations deep into Dad's soft tissue and looking like Linda Blair getting ready to spin her head around while he's at it. I swear I wouldn't have been surprised to walk back into the living room to find Dad clutching at his vitals. Dad thinks he spoils Jordan—worries all the time that he'll grow up soft—but all he does, really, is give him about two more chances than he ever gave me before he sends him to his room. Jordan doesn't appear to be growing up soft. I mention it because I have taken to hauling him on some training runs on this special bike seat Shelly custom-made in metal shop for my birthday, which isn't till July. She gave it to me early, along with some weighted webbed gloves for swimming and leaded innersoles for my running shoes to accompany the ankle weights, as an edge against my old enemy, gravity. *Use these day and night,* the card read, *right up to race day, and you'll feel so light you'll fly through Yukon Jack's.* When I step onto the scales in my street clothes these days, I've gained about ten pounds. But I'll tell you, if I swam with a bowling ball around my neck and a railroad tie across my shoulders, it couldn't approach the pain in the butt it is to have Jordan Brewster strapped onto his special seat on the back of my bike. "Will we be speeding up soon?" he queries on the really steep hills. "Don't you think we should hurry?" "When's dinner?" "This is no fun if you don't talk to me."

Call me when you're doing a show on fratricide, Lar.

Short entry today. There will be more of these because my training schedule is heating up. Several weeks back Mr. S said now is the time to get in distances most people would only travel by car. The more miles I log into my body's computer now, the more invulnerable I'll be on race day.

I feel kind of guilty because I stopped working out with the CFU swimming team. I told Mr. S it's because I'm really backed up on homework, but I'm sure he knows my study habits better than that—that it's because of what he told me about himself. It's costing me, because I've been swimming after work during open lap swim, and I can't push myself like I could when I thought Ian Wyrack might dismember me after every repeat. But I'll tell you, Lar, it's all I can do to face Mr. S in Journalism class. He knows it and gives me wide berth, I think. God, maybe I am a bigot. I miss him, and I want to make it right, but then I get so goddamn *angry* at him when I think of what he is. I know it's wrong, but I can't make myself fix it.

Outta here.

Your eyes and ears in the Northwest,

Bo

"**H**ey, Ironman."

Bo glances up from his milk shake to see Ian Wyrack and three swimmers from CFU kicking snow off their boots at the entrance to Doc's Drive-Inn.

"Yeah?"

"Where you been?" He approaches unthreateningly. "Haven't seen you at morning workouts lately."

"I've been working out in the evenings. Got behind at school. What do you care? I thought you didn't want my skin touching the same water as yours."

Wyrack smiles. "Yeah, well, there is that, but to tell the truth, my times *were* getting better."

Bo takes a slow drink of his shake, watching Wyrack's friends settle into the booth behind him. Ron Koch, the butterflier who stood up for Bo back in the early morning parking lot, smiles and gives a little wave. Bo looks back to Wyrack. "Man, were you put on earth just to mess with my head?"

Wyrack places his hands on the table and leans forward. "Don't get me wrong, Ironman. I don't like you any better than I ever did. You're *weak*, and I hate that, but competition at Nationals this year is going to be tough, and I could use the push. So if you want to come back, don't let me stop you."

"You really know how to make a guy feel wanted, know that? What do you mean I'm weak?"

Wyrack sneers. "Well, your little dyke girlfriend does your heavy work—"

"Hey, that was—"

"You walked out on your high-school football team when they were counting on you, man. That's weak."

Bo flares. "Hey, I quit football because—Wait a minute. How'd you know I quit football? You hotdog university jocks don't follow our football team."

"Let's just say I've learned a lot about you since the first day you showed up at the pool, Ironman. And everything I've learned points to weak."

Bo wants to ask who Wyrack has been talking to, but he knows. "Yeah, well, how weak is touching you out on nineteen of twenty hundred-yard frees?"

"I didn't say you don't have some talent." Wyrack points to his temple. "I said you were *weak*. I'm gonna love taking your money, schoolboy, I'm gonna love taking your money."

Bo and Shelly move through the doorway into Nak's group. "Wyrack said something strange the other day."

"There's a surprise. What did he say?"

"He said he was going to love taking my money."

No response.

"I thought he was baiting me like he always does, but I don't have any idea what he meant. He's an asshole, but I don't think he's a stick-up man. Hell, look at the car he drives. His parents must be loaded."

Shelly glances back toward the door. "I wonder where Mr. Nak is. He's almost never late. I—"

Bo grips her bicep.

"What?"

"You know something about this."

"What are you talking about? Know something about what?"

"I say, 'Wyrack's going to love taking my money,' and you look around for Mr. Nak. I haven't known you that long relative to all of world history, but I've known you long enough to know that means you're up to your overdeveloped gluteus in this."

"Jeez, Brewster, are you paranoid or what? I've just never seen Mr. Nak be late before."

Bo's eyes narrow. "Did you make a bet with him?"

"Mr. Nak?"

"Mr. Wyrack. How much?"

"What are you . . . ?"

"Come on, Shelly, you bet him. How much?"

Shelly hesitates. "Five."

"Five bucks? Shit, that's no big deal. The way Wyrack was talking I thought—"

"Five hundred."

"What?"

Shelly draws a five and two zeros in the air. "Five hundred, Bo. I bet him five hundred dollars you'd beat him and his bozos in Yukon Jack's."

"Shelly!" The heads of the group members turn as one to stare as Bo and Shelly drop into their seats. "What the hell were you thinking about?" he whispers loudly. "Where are you going to get five hundred dollars?"

"I'm not," she says back. "They'll never take you. I watched you guys up at the pool a couple of weeks back. You beat Wyrack every race."

The door clicks shut behind Mr. Nak, and Shuja says, "Looks like we got us a anger management situation developin' here, Mr. Nak. I think she's gonna take him out."

"Swimming's my best part," Bo says to her, ignoring all around him. "Lonnie Gerback is biking for them. As soon as swimming season's over, he'll be hammering out seventy miles a day. That guy wins *real* bike races."

"Then you'll have to stay close and kill 'em on the run," Shelly says. "Bo, you're training like a madman. There's no way they'll be ready for you."

"But *why* would you bet him five hundred dollars?"

Shelly drops her gaze, obviously embarrassed. "I guess I need a little more anger management," she says. "He baited me, then threatened to pull out of the race if it wasn't worth his time."

"So you decided five hundred clams for a few hours' work would be about right?"

"Actually, he picked the amount." Shelly looks up and smiles. "But look, Bo, he'll have to cut it three ways. If you win, you'll only have to cut it two."

Bo turns to face Mr. Nak. "I think I'm ready to graduate, Mr. Nak."

"Is that right?" Nak says. "What makes you think so?"

"Because I'm not going to kill her right in front of you all."

Nak smiles. "Even if you kill her in the privacy of your own home, or even jus' maim her good, you still need work."

Elvis explodes. "How much longer we gotta put up with this punk? Shit, he don't need anger management. He's too much of a wuss to ever get good and pissed. So what the hell if he called Redmond an asshole? That's like callin' Shuja black, or Hudgie fucked up, or"—and he nods at Shelly—"Wonder Woman a dyke."

Shelly says, "Up yours, Elvis. Mr. Nak, why don't you get rid of this creep? He's never going to have any more manners than he has right now."

"That's right," Elvis says, "stand up for your lover boy. I figured you out. You could be a dyke and still fall for this wuss because nobody knows if he's a boy or a girl. That how you're keeping your cover, Wonder Woman?"

Blood rushes to Bo's face and he turns his chair to face Elvis square on. "Tell you what, Rock 'n' Roll King, any time you want to find out, I'll be more than happy to settle this privately." He wants the words back as soon as they are spent.

Elvis leaps to his feet. "Hell with privately! How 'bout right here! Right now!"

Bo is also up. "Fine with me!"

Almost without notice, Nak slips to the floor and glides between them. "You buckaroos are forgettin' somethin', ain't ya? On my ranch nobody's ass gets kicked."

Shuja says, "Oooh. Come on, Mr. Nak. Let 'em go. Let's get some anger out here to manage."

Elvis turns. "You want some of this, too, nigger?"

Now Shuja rises. He is fluid lean, muscular in the way of a thoroughbred. He points the index finger of his right hand at Elvis's chest and says, "Elvis, my man, you done made a big mistake."

Nak moves between the two of them. "I'll say it one more time," he says in low, even tones. "Ain't gonna be no ass kickin' here. It may help you boys to know that I got me a number of black belts in a number of disciplines, an' while I'd never hurt ya, if you keep this up, I'll embarrass you."

"Hey, no white punk calls me a nigger," Shuja says. "I *got* to hurt 'im."

"Tell you what," Nak says. "Let's sit down an' see if we can work this out. If not, you guys can set your place an' time an' do your binniss."

Elvis and Shuja glare at each other over Nak's head, each refusing to make the first move in retreat. Bo has gratefully taken his seat.

Again in his low tone, Mr. Nak says, "Either way, it ain't gonna happen here."

Shuja is the first to move. "We discuss this later, white boy."

"I'll be there," Elvis says, backing slowly toward his seat.

Nak takes a deep breath, and walks slowly toward the board. "Lotta damn name callin' goin' on in here. Seems like my earballs have been flooded with 'nigger, Chinaman, dyke, white boy, white punk,' just in recent memory. 'Asshole' is a staple in these parts. What's all this about, you think?"

Hudgie's hand shoots up.

"Talk to me, Hudge."

"Make that rock 'n' roll dude take back that I'm fucked up."

Nak watches Hudgie's desperate stare and his eyes go soft. "Sticks and stones may break my bones," he says, "but names will break my heart."

Elvis's head turns, ever so slightly, also catching Hudgie's desperation. "Hey, Hudge, you ain't fucked up. I wasn't pissed at you. I shouldn't of said that. You ain't fucked up, man."

A satisfied look crosses Hudgie's face, and he gives a quick nod. "Certainly not," he says. "I'm certainly not fucked up."

"I want y'all to hear somethin'," Nak says. "I know you think all these words you're usin' on one another make ya tough. But ya know what I hear? I don't hear tough at all. I hear scared."

Elvis snorts and looks at his feet, shaking his head in disgust.
"He ain't scared now," Shuja says, "but he gonna be."

Nak puts up a hand. "Jus' gimme this time, okay, Shu?"

Shuja nods, and is quiet.

"Cain't think of a reason to put a name on a man's skin color, or a woman's muscles, or"—and he looks directly at Bo—"somebody's sexual preference, or any part of a human being that just *is*, 'cept for fear. Fear's the only reason. Now I'm gonna make some guesses, an' what I want you all to do is just listen to 'em an' be quiet, an' think about 'em, an' you can tell me I'm full of shit later."

Nak walks toward Shuja and crouches down a couple of feet from him. "I'm guessin' it ain't real cool to be black around these parts. You don't have a lot of company. If you want to go out with a girl who ain't your same color, you got to worry that she'll push you away without tellin' you why—or you got to worry about her folks puttin' the kibosh on it an' givin' you some reason you know is a lie. You have to worry that nobody'll tell you the truth. You can't let anybody see what that does to you, because then you have to give up your 'don't give a shit' attitude, which is keepin' you afloat." He nods slowly. "Plenty to be scared of there, but no way to say it."

He moves to Elvis. "Hell to be poor, ain't it, Elvis? To have parents that jus' don't take care of things, so you're left to do it. To know you could be a fine athlete or an A student or just real good at whatever you try, but you cain't do any of that because you're embarrassed about what you ain't got. 'Don't give a shit' attitude works there, too, but all them thoughts in your head about what people are thinkin' an' whether you're gonna be able to take care of things while you're watchin' 'em fall apart, well, them thoughts gonna turn to anger. You're gonna have to find people lower'n you to keep your head above water. So the muscle lady's a dyke an' the black kid's a nigger, I'm a Chinaman, an' the put-together-lookin' kid's a wuss."

Elvis looks to the side. "Fuck you."

"An' when somebody gets close to the truth, you say fuck 'em."

"Man, I don't have to listen to this. . . ."

"No," Nak says, "you don't. But you should. Come on, Elvis, tell us what's really botherin' you."

"Fuck it," Elvis says. "Ain't nobody here cares."

"You don't know that."

Elvis stares at a spot inches from his face. "It ain't nothin'."

"Then say it. If it ain't nothin', say it."

FEBRUARY 10

Dear Larry,

I've been watching miracles, Lar. Things almost blew the other day in Nak's Pack. Elvis was coming at me and Shelly, then at Shuja. Half the group was standing up ready to take on the other half, when Mr. Nak stood up like some kind of Will Rogers with a giant lasso and did a giant rope trick—a rope miracle. Instead of looking at our anger, he got us talking about things we're scared of. And no one could get loose, not even Elvis, because Mr. Nak was right: It's fear that's crazy in the world, not anger. But the more fear there is, the more anger it takes to cover it. I swear to God, I'm starting to get it.

Elvis was in a rage, but somehow Mr. Nak worked him around to saying what was really wrong. And you know what it was? He's afraid he's just like his old man—and that he's going to have to live the life his old man is living. Elvis had *tears* in his eyes, no shit, Lar.

Mr. Nak kept pushing him to say what was really wrong, and Elvis fought him off pretty good for a while, but Mr. Nak held on like a wise, gentle pit bull who won't let go until he sinks his teeth into the truth.

Finally, Elvis said, "I'm takin' care of my family now," and his lips was quivering all over the place.

Mr. Nak said, "Your daddy ain't back?"

Elvis shook his head and said, "Only I ain't takin' care

112

of them kids no better than he was. Hell, I bloodied
Fabian's lip." And then tears were dripping off his nose.
"He's my little brother and I bloodied his lip. He looked at
me like . . . Well, like I was a monster or somethin'." And
then his voice got real quiet, and he said, "Like I was my
old man."

Mr. Nak said, "Damn," and he walked around behind
Elvis and put a hand on his shoulder and said, "We've let
this go too far. Like I said before, there's people to hep
with that stuff. You come on down to the office with me
when group's over an' we'll see what we can do." He
stood up to include the rest of us and said, "Pay attention.
You're gettin' to see where some of this nastiness comes
from."

Elvis said, "Man, I gotta get outta here," and Mr. Nak
took him into his little office and pulled the blinds. Then
he came back out and said, "I'd like y'all to call a
moratorium on the ass kickin' around here for a while,
least till we can sort some of this out. That okay with
everbody?"

There were grunts.

"How 'bout you, Shu?" he asked. "Seems like you're a
key cowpoke in this one."

"I'm solid, Mr. Nak. He bes' don't be callin' me nigger
no more, though."

"Yeah," Mr. Nak said. "I think it's a real bad idea to
call you that. But I think maybe Elvis is gettin' a little
better idea where his attitude comes from."

Mr. Nak let the group go early, but he said, "Mr.
Brewster, you wanna hang around a second?"

My stomach jumped a bit, but I said okay.

When the room had cleared out, he asked me to sit
down, and I did. "When I was listin' the names, Mr.
Brewster, I left one out."

I asked which one.

He said, "Faggot."

I was stunned, Lar. I couldn't remember calling
anybody that, and I said so.

He said, "Maybe I heard it because it's so loud inside your head."

I just stared. I really didn't know what he was talking about.

He said, "I'm talking about Mr. Serbousek."

Blood flushed into my head like the septic tank below the World Trade Center.

Mr. Nak said, "Looks like you do know what I'm talkin' about. Why would you turn on a man stickin' hisself out that far for you?"

I couldn't speak.

"He let you work out with his team, he took you under his wing at school—hell, he's half the reason Redmond can't get his hands on you the way he wants—he's there to walk through any particular hell you wanna walk through, an' you turn your back on him 'cause he tells you the truth. You know, young Brewster, maybe I oughta go on an' graduate you out of this group. I don't mind workin' with a man's anger, but I have a hard time workin' with a man who turns his back on his friends. I think it's time for you to step up, or I'm through wasting my time."

I hung my head; I couldn't bear having Mr. Nak mad at me.

He said, "Yeah. Shame on you."

"How'd you know?" I said finally.

"He told me. Hell, boy, his feelins is hurt."

I was quiet a few seconds more, and Mr. Nak got up to leave. I said, "Wait," and he turned. "If I'm gonna do this, I'm gonna need some help."

"What kind of hep you need?" He still felt real cold.

"Well, I just can't make him being homo . . . gay . . . okay with me."

"It don't need to be okay with you," Mr. Nak said. "It needs to be okay with him."

"Yeah, okay," I said. "But I still need a way to act. Now that I know it, I can't pretend I don't."

"What's your problem with it?"

"I don't know. It's just that I've always been told to be careful—"

"You think it means something about *you*?"

"I don't know."

"Well, let me give you a little schoolin'," he said. "Heterosexuals wreak a heap more havoc in this world than homosexuals do. Hell, you got nothin' to be careful *of*. Teachers ain't allowed to mess with kids under any circumstances. It's got nothin' to do with sexual preference, it's got to do with age an' position. Lionel Serbousek walks with as much integrity as any man I know. What he does in the privacy of his own home is totally apart from his professional life. You *have* to know that, Brewster. If you've got a brain in your head, you have to know that. Hell, you bitch about your daddy—all set in his ways—an' here you are, doin' the very thing you bitch about most. Maybe I oughta take you in the office an' let you compare notes with Elvis."

He was right, Lar. Completely right. But I still couldn't just let it go. I could lie and say I would, but I knew I'd have to face Mr. S and he'd know if something was still wrong. Finally I said, "I think it has something to do with the picture in my head. I don't know."

Mr. Nak smiled then, and I was really glad, because I didn't think I'd ever see him smile at me again. He shook his head like I was some kind of pitiful puppy somebody left out in the rain, and he said, "Brewster, do you sit around thinkin' about what it looked like when your momma and daddy conceived you? You know, like right when they were doin' it?"

Well, shit, Lar, what kid in his right mind would do that? I said, "Hey, I'm not some kind of pervert."

"That's not what I asked. I asked if you picture your momma and daddy doin' the nasty thing."

I said of course not.

"Why not?"

"They're my *mom* and *dad*, for chrissake."

He said, "Well, you seem to pass judgment on

somebody's sexuality by what it looks like inside your head. I thought you might have included them on that, too. What about your grandparents?"

"Nope," I said. "I don't picture my grandparents making love."

"So how come your family gets to operate on a different standard than Mr. Serbousek?"

I said, "Okay, I get it. Actually, it helps. It helps a lot."

He said, "What is it you get?"

"You're saying, don't think about it if it bothers me."

"Thank you, young feller. You just bought yourself another day in Anger Management. Woulda been cheap at twice the price," and he turned toward his office.

I probably don't need to tell you I was so goddamn relieved I couldn't believe it. Losing Mr. S was one of the worst things in that ever happened to me, and I didn't even know it because I was stuck in my own stupid head.

And when I go back, I'm not just going to walk into the pool like nothing happened. I'm going to tell him what I did and what I was thinking. He told me some important things about fathers and sons that night, and I trashed them when he told me the truth about himself. Mr. Nak is right: shame on me. But I'm going back to him like a Stotan. He'd be proud of me for that. Gotta go, Lar. I'm going to have to cook this crow for a long time so it'll slide down a little easier.

Ever so *humbly* yours,

The Ex Gay Basher

"Mom, would you tell me something?" Bo sits on the counter next to the kitchen sink, eating watermelon balls from the fruit salad nearly as fast as Ellen Brewster can scoop them out of the heart of the melon.

"Yes, dear, I will tell you something: If you eat one more of those melon balls before dinner I will weld your Ironman's hands together."

Bo plunks the melon ball destined for his mouth back into the bowl. "Jeez," he says, "what ever happened to 'Wait till your dad gets home'?"

"It'd be a long wait," she says. "What do you want me to tell you, honey?"

"Why didn't you and Dad make it?"

Ellen's eyes narrow as she wipes her hands slowly on her apron. "Are you and your girlfriend having trouble?"

Bo shakes his head. "No, no trouble. It's just . . . I just wondered. . . ."

"If it will last?"

Bo smiles. "Yeah, I guess so."

"You're pretty excited about her, aren't you?"

Blood flows into his cheeks. "Jeez, Mom. I'll ask the questions, okay?"

"Okay. You want to know why your father and I didn't make it." She slowly scoops out more melon balls, moving the salad bowl out of Bo's reach and thinking. "We didn't make it because I was weak."

"What do you mean?"

"I mean when I first met your father in high school, I was

so much in love I'd have done anything to keep him. I simply adored him, and that didn't change. He was handsome and athletic and all the girls in my class envied me. When I think back, I wonder if I didn't stay with him through his moods just so one of those other girls wouldn't get him."

"He had those moods back then?"

"He certainly did, but I ignored them or, worse, I attributed them to his masculinity; I was actually attracted to them."

"God, Mom, isn't that sick?"

"Probably. But if so, I'm afraid it's epidemic." Ellen begins to set dishes on the table. "Look, Bo, it's really easy to turn up your nose at men like your father, men who think that being in control means controlling everyone else, but most of them come by it honestly. Your dad couldn't have occupied that spot in our family if I hadn't allowed it, if I hadn't occupied mine."

"You sound like it's your fault that Dad was an—"

Ellen raises a carrot peeler. "Hold out your tongue and let me whittle it to a point. I'm not saying that at all. I'm saying I have responsibility for what I allow in my life and the lives of my children. Sometimes people behave the way they do just because they can. If I hadn't allowed your father's behavior in my life from the beginning, he would have changed it, or we'd have parted ways earlier."

Bo leans back. "Do you ever wish that?"

"Every day of my life." She sets a handful of silverware on the edge of the table and sits. "Bo, do you remember those months, back in grade school, when your father banished you to your room?"

Bo snorts. "Do you remember where you were when President Kennedy was shot?"

"That's what I thought. Why is it you and I have never talked about that? Why haven't you ever brought it up?"

"You slapped my face, remember?"

Tears rim Ellen's eyes and a slight, involuntary moan escapes her. "Yes. I remember." She moves the short distance to where

Bo is seated, sliding her arms around his neck. "Oh, Bo, we . . ." but she chokes.

"Aw, come on, Mom. It's all right. I forgot about it till you brought it up. I don't need to talk about it. It's over, a long time ago. Come on, Mom."

She shakes her head. "I need to talk about it, even if you don't. Bo, that incident, along with some others like it, is the shame of my life. I can forgive myself for almost everything, but those times when I just stood by and let him take you apart just bring me to my knees."

"Mom, I survived, okay? It wasn't your fault."

"What did you *think* of me, Bo?"

"I didn't think anything. I just thought Dad was an asshole and I wasn't going to let him win."

"I don't believe that."

"Well, it's true," Bo says. "I never thought you were responsible for what Dad did to me."

"I *wasn't* responsible for what he did to you. I was responsible for what I didn't do. Look, honey, if you're not mad at me for that, then it's real possible you have a dangerously distorted view of any woman's capabilities. If that's true, you'd best reexamine it, or you'll run into problems with your girlfriend— or *any* girlfriend, for that matter. Problems that you can't imagine."

"What does this have to do with Shelly?"

"It doesn't have anything to do with Shelly. It has to do with you and how you react to the world. I'm your mother. You had better deal with your anger at me."

Bo's mind flashes to himself as a little boy, sitting on the edge of his bed, hating her guts for slapping his face and for defending his father, and a cold whirlwind runs up his spine.

Ellen catches his look. She says, "That's what I'm talking about."

"Jesus, I did . . . I mean, I was mad. Really mad. I felt like you left me. I remember thinking you of all people should know . . ."

Ellen lowers her eyes.

"But it's okay, Mom. I mean, I forgave you a long time ago. It wasn't your fault. There was nothing you could—"

"Stop it," she says softly. "Don't ever say there's nothing I could have done. That diminishes me." She looks up and smiles through the tears. "And don't worry about me crying. It's okay for me to cry about this. It's something to be cried about. You may have forgiven me, Bo, but you can't erase the experience, and neither can I."

FEBRUARY 14

Dear Larry,

It's Valentine's Day, Lar, and I think ol' Cupid got slapped around a little at my house today. I had a little blip in the back of my mind that said I should check out with Mom why her and Dad's marriage got derailed. I ended up getting a five-credit graduate course in marital and family dysfunction.

The scary part was that after she finished beating herself to death for not standing up to my father during his Neo-Pleistocene Hitler period, she described all the feelings that got her hooked up with him, and they were *exactly the same feelings I have for Shelly*. Aaagghh! (Don't get me wrong. Shelly is nothing like my dad, but I have the same blind, deaf, and dumb, brain-numbing feelings my mother had for my dad. I see her pumping iron or in her aerobics class, so powerful, yet so soft, and I'd do anything for her. Anything, Lar, do you hear me?) Mom told me that if I didn't do anything else before I get out of high school, I'd better discover the difference between falling in love and loving somebody. It wasn't my dad who was a lie; her feelings were the lie, and what she did because of them. And I have them, too. I thought I'd save myself some research and just ask her how she figured it out, but she

120

said, "If I had figured it out, Bo, would I be spending my life alone?"

Shit, Lar. Think I should talk to Shelly about this?

Outta here for a long run,

Tinman

"I guess I've been pretty much of an asshole," Bo says as Lion drops a stack of Journalism assignments into his backpack.

"We've missed you at the morning workouts," Lion says back.

Bo runs his thumbnail along the edge of Lion's desk. "I couldn't face you."

"Couldn't stand to think of me as a queer, huh?"

"It's not that," Bo says, "it's just that . . . Yeah, it is that. Or was."

"So what changed your mind?"

"Talking with Mr. Nak, mostly. He made it pretty clear whose problem this is."

Lion says, "Nak's good that way."

Bo nods. "So do you think I could start working out with you guys again? In the mornings, I mean?"

"Far as I'm concerned, you never stopped. Wrote it off as a midtraining breather."

Bo takes a deep breath and the words fall out in a gravity dump. "Coach, I'm sorry, I really am. I mean *really* sorry. I don't know what . . . if I ever . . . I should have known. . . . I mean we can still have pizza and everything. I just . . ."

Lion raises his hand in protest and says, "Stop. Tell you what, buddy. If you learned anything about prejudice—about bigotry—and you pass it on, it was worth a few weeks of losing you, okay? I won't lie; those weeks weren't easy. It really hurts"—and he pounds his chest with a flat hand—"it *crushes*, to have someone as special as you turn away from me because of something that's just a part of me. But if you learned a truth from it, and if you're stronger or smarter—well, that's what I got into the teaching business for, and I got my money's worth." He slaps Bo on the shoulder. "So we don't need to talk about it anymore. We're even up, and you've got big-time Stotan work to do."

VALENTINE'S AFTERNOON

Whooee Larry,

I feel *good*! The world's tilted right on its axis again. I'm cool with Mr. S and I'm cool with Mr. Nak, and I'm the hottest number since Johnny Depp as far as Shelly's concerned.

I need to tell you something about working out, Lar, about being a triathlete. Lately I've been thinking maybe God was behind my self-imposed banishment from team sports, rather than Redmond, because this kind of training feels almost spiritual. There were times in the fall as I hammered over the rolling hills outside town on my bike, pushing my body past the wind chill, and the agony of being fileted on that razor blade of a seat, and the searing burn in my thighs and calves, and the unrelenting ache across the back of my shoulders, to a place where pain simply didn't matter and I could feel the *mechanics* of my body: feel muscle move bone and air swirl through my lungs into my bloodstream. It sounds hokey, but it's true. I feel the same way swimming. When I flip into the third turn on the fifteenth of a set of twenty one-hundreds, neck and neck with Wyrack, and my lungs want to burst and my triceps and deltoids threaten to melt and I know it's never going to end, somehow I call up this *power*, and it feels like hate, and it feels like love, and I simply pull ahead.

It's a dance, Lar. The rhythm of my feet pounding the pavement or the hard snow, the steely repetitions forcing the weights to the beat of Seger or Springsteen, the hum of the tires as I hammer out another mile, the slapping of my hands on the water in perfect drum cadence—it's a dance. And I want to tell people, but only a few can hear

122

because if you haven't taken your body or your brain or your spirit down that road, you are deaf to it. So I'm telling you, Lar, because even though it's hard to picture you in serious workout gear, you listen to everything.

Shelly can hear it; that's one reason I love her. When she's lifting or running or dancing, there's nothing and no one else in the world—it all belongs to her. Seeing the way she loves her body makes me have to love it, too. I feel bad for people who can't find that rhythm; for guys like Elvis, who'll never be jocks because they have the same picture of athletics as Redmond has, only Redmond loves them and Elvis hates them; for guys like Hudge, who are unaware they even have a body.

Speaking of Hudge, there's true tragedy there, Lar. Rumors flew all over school today about him. I'll tell you about it when I'm not drop-dead tired. I gotta catch a nap, then put in an hour or so cleaning up down at the newspaper before the Anger Management Valentine's Day party. (Can you believe *that*?) We were supposed to have it this morning, but Don the janitor came in to tell us Mr. Nak was taking care of an emergency and that we'd have to come back this evening. Turned out the emergency was out at Hudge's place. Tell you more when I know more. Hey, I'm a drooling-all-over-the-page goner.

Zzzzzzzzzzzzzz,

Bo

Don the janitor bangs down the panic bar with his broomstick and kicks the side entrance to the school open, allowing Bo and Shelly in from the bitter cold. Don bends at the waist in an exaggerated bow and says, "Happy Valentine's Day, you angry young lovers." The angry young lovers carry brightly decorated boxes filled with valentine cards for each of the other members of the group, to be distributed among similar boxes once the party begins. Neither has participated in this ritual since sixth grade, but Nak's "Mandatory Love Fest" is exactly that, and even though the group meeting was canceled this morning due to an emergency, everyone is present for the new meeting time.

"*Damn!*" Shuja says, plopping his box on the long worktable at the rear of the room, "I should be with my woman. This *Valentine*'s Day. She need to be with her lover boy."

"She probably is," Elvis says, and for a brief moment Shuja is caught between possible responses.

He chooses one appropriate for the occasion. "This here Valentine's Day," he says again. "Be good to me, Rock 'n' Roll. Don' be makin' me feel all blue."

A heavy, new, and otherwise nondescript sophomore group member named Robert Brown shakes his head and says, "Man, this sucks. Old Lady Stevens said I had to come to this shit in the mornings. I came this morning. That ought to be enough." His comment plays to general agreement, which mutes itself as Mr. Nak walks into the room.

"Ever one accounted for?" he asks with a quick smile. "Looks like it," he says in answer to his own question.

Someone says, "Except for Hudge."

"Hudge is takin' a few days off," Mr. Nak says. "Boy needs some rest." He looks far off, then shakes his head quickly.

Shelly asks, "Is Hudgie okay, Mr. Nak? There were rumors about him today. I mean, that's why we didn't have group this morning, right, because you went out to his place?"

Nak's eyes narrow as he decides what should and can be said. "Yeah, Hudge is okay. Restin' up in the hospital. Wouldn't be too bad an idea if a few of you stopped up to see him after a day or so." He pauses again, thinking. "Guess it's best y'all know what happened. He's one of us."

The group waits quietly. Shelly was right. Rumors had flown all over school that Hudgie Walters went crazy, that he'd been hurt and was in intensive care, that he'd shot his father. "Best forget most of what you heard today," Nak says. "I got a call from the police about six o'clock this mornin', askin' if I'd be willin' to run on out to the Walters place to help calm down a situation. When I got there, I found Hudge on the front porch in his pj's with a pup in his lap. Hudge was talkin' to it an' kinda rockin' back an' forth the way he does, only it didn't take long to see that pup was deader'n Old Yeller. Hudge was kinda singin' to it, sayin' he was sorry, an' there was a policeman an' some social worker standin' several feet away. Each time one of 'em tried to move in on him, Hudge'd start screamin' loud enough to scare 'em right back.

"They told me they took his pa off because he'd greeted the cops with a shotgun when they showed up to see what all the commotion that the neighbors reported was about. His momma was inside somewhere, locked in a room. So the cop asked me to see if I could maybe get Hudge to come with him; said Hudge'd been hollerin' my name.

"Anyway, I walk over an' kneel down beside him, an' ask if maybe he wants to go in the house an' get somethin' warm on, an' he tells me no, that he killed his dog. So I ask him how he done that, an' he says he forgot to feed 'im. I tell 'im, 'Hudge, you cain't kill a critter forgettin' to feed it once,' an' he says, 'Oh, yes, you can, if your daddy's gonna shoot 'im if you don't take care of 'im, you can.' "

Nak's gaze drops to the table. He is visibly shaken. "Well, I look down at that little feller, an' sure enough he's bleedin' all over Hudge's lap. Been shot deader'n hell. When I try to take him away from Hudge, he starts screamin' an' gettin' all crazy on me, so I say he can bring him right along, but we *are* gonna go on in an' get him into somethin' warm."

The group is riveted to Nak's story, staring in disbelief.

"Anyway," Nak continues, "I convince him we got to give this animal a proper burial, an' we go out back an' dig under the snow into the frozen dirt an' plant him in the garden, an' I say a few words I think will get the job done for Hudge, an' Hudge just keeps sayin' he's sorry as he covers the little dickens with snow an' dirt. Then he rides with me up to the hospital— to the psych ward—an' the social worker gets him all checked in, an' I think they probably had to sedate him some when I left because he was gettin' perty wild agin.''

Nak looks up at the group. ''Anyway, that's why I was a no-show this mornin' an' why y'all had to come in here tonight.''

Shawn Reed, another relatively new group member says, ''Why couldn't we have just canceled? Ain't our fault this Hudgie guy's got a crazy dad.''

Shuja shakes his head. ''Man, you *cold*.''

Elvis is out of his chair. ''Reed, you shut your mouth. One more word an' you're dust.''

Reed starts to respond, but Nak stands. ''Guys, I ain't got a lot of energy left to deal with this. Sit down, Elvis. Please.'' He raises a hand, and Elvis sits.

''You're right, Mr. Reed. It ain't our fault Hudge's got a crazy dad. Ain't Hudge's fault, either. It's just the way it is. But Hudge's one of us, an' when one of us goes down, the rest of us get in on it whether we like it or not. Once you know somethin', you can't unknow it.''

Nak sits back down on the table. ''You know, ol' Hudge takes quite a beatin' around this school. Everbody's always wonderin' what's wrong with him, why he acts so crazy, where them wild rages of his come from. Well, now you know, an' you know all kinds of folks are going to be tauntin' 'im an' pointin' an' such when he comes back. This one'll hit the papers for sure. What I'd appreciate is if none of that tauntin' came from inside this room. When a guy's wounded, you need to huddle up on 'im.''

Shelly says, ''Don't worry, Mr. Nak. We'll huddle up.''

''*Man*,'' Shuja says. ''His daddy shoot his dog?''

''That he did,'' Nak says. ''So let's git along with this here Valentine's celebration. Y'all bring your boxes?''

CHAPTER 12

Dear Larry,

Man, Lar, I think Valentine's Day could take on a different meaning for me from now on. I told you earlier Mr. Nak was called out to something important this morning, so Nak's Pack met this evening instead. It seemed strange that he didn't just cancel it instead of messing up everyone's schedule, including his own, but he said Valentine's Day could be *the* most important holiday for us, since it's supposed to be a celebration of people's good feelings for one another, and this culture doesn't seem to be able to make a significant distinction between those feelings and anger most of the time. Otherwise, why would so many people be getting whacked on in the name of love?

Hey, man, Mr. Nak has made stranger points.

About three weeks ago he tells us each to begin constructing a Valentine's box, you know, like we used to make in grade school; said he wanted them all fixed up like we did back then so he could give a prize for the best one. Don't think he didn't catch some crap for *that*. You think it's easy for a guy like Elvis to be caught toting a red-and-white box covered with crepe-paper hearts? As I remember, Elvis mentioned something about that at the time, but Mr. Nak said to think of it like trying to graduate high school without your math credits. You couldn't graduate Anger Management without your Valentine's credits. He said it as a joke, but you got the feeling you didn't want to be a no-show for the Anger Management Valentine's Day extravaganza.

He said we were also to bring a valentine for each member of the group. "You don't have to write some earth-shakin' thing that'd turn back a thunderin' herd of raging longhorns," he told us, "just somethin' decent that's true."

On the surface that may not seem like such a tall order, Lar, until you remember the last time some of these guys said anything nice about anybody was about two past lives ago.

Since I worried that Mr. Nak might make us read the cards aloud, I gave Shelly two valentines: one privately that said how I really feel about her, and one for the group that said I like the way she hardly ever puts anybody down. A guy wants to stay safe with his feelings of romance, huh, Lar? Would you want to give these guys ammo?

Mr. Nak never did make us read anything aloud, though. After we distributed the cards to the individual boxes, he told us about Hudge, who's in the psychiatric unit at Sacred Heart Hospital in Spokane. Mr. Nak got a call from the Clark Fork police about six o'clock this morning, asking if he would come out to Hudge's house to help calm down a situation. Seems Hudge's dad shot his puppy because Hudge forgot to feed it. Killed him, Lar. This guy shot a kid's dog just to teach him a lesson. And I thought my old man had a corner on hardass. When Mr. Nak got out there, Hudge was sitting on his porch in the freezing cold with nothing on but his pj's, apologizing to this dead puppy because he caused him to get shot. Ol' Hudge wasn't even mad at his dad. He thought it was his fault because his dad warned him when Hudge brought it home that he'd shoot it if Hudge didn't take care of it.

Hudge's dad was charged with discharging a firearm within city limits. Can you believe that? It's okay to kill your dog, just don't do it with a firearm inside city limits. And *Hudge was screaming at the cops to leave his dad alone while they hauled him off!* I mean, he didn't even know it was his dad's fault, Lar; Hudge thought *he* killed the dog. I think that's how badly you can be tricked if you can't find a way to stand up for yourself.

"Guess this couldn't have happened on a better day for teachin' us about love," Mr. Nak said after he told us the story. "I heard Hudge's dad say three times while they was haulin' him off that he did it for the kid's own good. Damn. Loved the boy so much he was willing to kill his dog just to teach him a lesson. Anybody wonder why the world seems like such a hellhole to that boy? You know that *sssss* sound he's always makin'? You know what that is? That's cigarettes burning the backs of his legs when he don't do his chores. Anybody wonder where his rage comes from?"

None of us wondered, Lar. At least no one said so.

"Reason I make Valentine's Day such a big deal for this group," Mr. Nak said, "is that it's the holiday for love, an' I'm just plain sick an' tired of all the lyin' done in the name of it. The kind of love Hudge gets can make a man so sick in his heart an' his mind he might just never recover. That kind of love is a lie, an' everybody in this room has a piece of that lie in his—or her—life. Y'all will have a lot less anger in you once you ferret those lies out."

Shelly started crying, Lar, crying hard—I think in response to Mr. Nak's story about Hudge. She was the only one to know the right question to ask. She asked how can we tell, said her life was so full of that kind of lie she'd never be able to sort it out.

Mr. Nak said, "If what's comin' from others don't make you feel better about yourself in the world, then it probably ain't good for you," he said. "An' if it ain't good for you, it ain't love. That ain't the whole story, but it'll do for a start." He paused a minute, then he said, "I asked y'all to write a little somethin' on a valentine card for everbody else here. I hope you spent a little time on it, thought of somethin' true to say."

I thought back on what I'd written and was pretty well satisfied—I hadn't slammed anybody, and I really did try to say something that was good and also true about each person. It wasn't easy in a few cases, because there are a few guys in there who don't talk much and when they do, they bitch.

"Before you look at your cards," Mr. Nak said, "I'm gonna read you a couplea Hudgie's. He gave this to me before they hauled him off." He reached behind his desk and hauled out an orange-and-blue five-gallon ice-cream tub monstrosity with all different color and size hearts plastered on it willy-nilly. "Want y'all to send Hudge's back in this. I'll take it up. If you made the mistake of mockin' or teasin' him for a joke, throw that one away, and I'll give you a blank one to fix." He looked up. "No questions asked."

Mr. Nak carefully removed the top from the carton, reached in, and drew out a handful of sealed envelopes, opening them one at a time. "This one's for you, Shelly," he said, holding the tiny ten-cent card face out for us to see a pig squeezing a large red heart. It said I SQUEAL WITH DELIGHT FOR YOU, VALENTINE.

Shelly smiled.

Mr. Nak said, "Hudge told me he had to hide the cash to buy these; said his daddy would've beat him if he caught him throwin' money away on such foolishness." Mr. Naks eyes narrowed. "So I want you to appreciate 'em. The price was high." He turned the card over and read. " 'Shelly. You're perty. And nice. If I was a guy who could have a girlfriend, you'd be who I'd want. Never mind that Ironman guy. Hudgie.' "

Shelly blushed, and Shuja said, "Oooh, Beauregard. You bein' dis*placed*." I didn't say anything. I was thinking about what it must be like to wish you were a guy who could have a girlfriend. Seems like that ought to be a right before bearing arms. That's almost too sad for words, Lar.

"This one here's for Elvis," Mr. Nak said, and I expected Elvis to look away or sneer or something, but he looked right at Mr. Nak. The picture was one of a bowling ball striking pins, with hearts flying every which way. The caption read YOU BOWL ME OVER, VALENTINE! Mr. Nak read

Hudgie's words off the back. "It says, 'Dear Mr. Rock 'n' Roll Guy. When somebody makes my head feel all hot and prickly by sayin' somethin' mean about me, sometimes you look like you're gonna hurt 'em. I like that. I don't think you're as mean as everybody thinks. Hudge.' "

Nobody laughed, Lar, because nobody ever knows how Elvis is going to respond, and the only one who would dare find out is Shuja, who wouldn't, most of the time. Mr. Nak read the rest of Hudge's cards, most of which were unintentionally funny, but with that same nice touch to them. He told Joey he wished he was Italian, too, so he could have pizza and a big family that liked him most of the time—although I think Joey only looks Italian, and there's plenty of question about the way his family likes him—and he told Mr. Nak he wished he was Japanese so he could talk like a cowboy, too. It was clear he didn't know a couple of the guys, because he got their names wrong, and what he said didn't fit, but you could see he'd put as much thought and effort into them as was possible for a guy living in hell.

When he finished, Mr. Nak held up a big, ugly, handmade card that was the same color as Hudge's box. It was addressed to the entire group. Mr. Nak read it, and he seemed very moved, which is unusual for Mr. Nak. It's unusual for Mr. Nak to show much of anything, really. "This one says, 'I know most of you wouldn't of knew who I was if I wasn't in angry management and I don't think a whole bunch of you will want to be my friend if this group gets broke up. But it's the safest place I been and Mr. Nak said we should be saying what's good, so this is it. I'm saying this is good because nobody almost ever hurts me here. Happy Valentines to angry management.' "

Then Mr. Nak gave us some time to read the rest of our cards while he went out and got some treats he'd brought: homemade ice cream and some cookies and cake. You could tell he made the cookies, because they were cut from what must be the one cookie cutter he has at home—a cowboy on a bucking bronco.

My valentines were pretty run-of-the-mill, Lar, except for one. Most of them said they thought I was a pretty good athlete, and that I didn't act too stuck-up like most jocks. That's a compliment in that crowd. Shelly must not have had the same worry about privacy I had, because her valentine said she had never even considered loving anybody before—that she thought it was stupid and risky—but that being with me was slowly changing that. She said she was excited about me, and she liked the way I touched her. Probably no need to tell you, Lar, that I squirmed majorly, due to a quick change in the status of my plumbing upon reading that.

But the unusual one came from Elvis. I'm not sure why I saved his until last—whether I was afraid of it, or whether I actually thought it might say something meaningful. Maybe I just wondered if it might contain a clue to how a guy like him survives a party like this. The card itself wasn't a valentine, but a plain white piece of cardboard like you might find in a new shirt. He had drawn a pair of running shoes, some swimming goggles, and a bicycle on the front, and it said IRONMAN. These were *good* drawings, Lar. I don't think they took him long to draw, I think he's just talented, but it touched me to have him recognize what was important to me.

Of course, that made me more afraid to turn it over in case he trashed me, but I did, and he didn't. It said, "I still don't like you very much, Ironman, but I guess I don't *not* like you all that much, either. Since most of the time I got nothing nice to say to anybody, I'll tell you something that should help you. Your daddy ain't your friend." He signed it "The King."

I glanced up at Elvis to find him staring at Shelly with a kind of surprised look on his face. He watched her a second, then stared back down at the card in his hand, which I assumed was from her. I remember for an instant thinking maybe she had written him something hot, but that was a stupid idea and I knew it wasn't true because of what my card from her had said.

I picked up my card from Elvis, walked over to his chair, and said, "I don't get it."

"What's to get?"

"This says my daddy ain't my friend. No offense, but it doesn't exactly take a genius to figure that out. How's it supposed to help me? I mean it's hardly news."

"Somethin' I seen," he says. "You wanna hear?"

I said yeah.

"Well, I was in your old man's store the other day— thought I might pick up some shoes for my little brother at my normal hundred percent discount. Anyway, your old man was talking to these college kids. One was the same guy you and your chick got into it with that night at the Drive-Inn. Your dad was showing these guys a bike out of a catalog—which made it easier for me to get the shoes—and he said he'd get it for them at no charge. They were laughin' and slappin' each other on the back like a couple of yuppie bite-asses, about what a sweet deal it was to get a five-thousand-dollar bike for free. I don't know exactly what kind of daddy you got, Ironman, other than what you've said in here, but I figure he's settin' it up for these guys to kick your ass for sure."

I asked Elvis if the bike in the catalog was black.

"Hell, I don't know, I didn't look. I just know it costs five thousand."

I know this bike, Lar, because I tried to make a deal with Dad last year to get one at dealer's price. I wanted it so bad I told him I'd make payments at a very high interest rate, and call him sir until it was paid off. It's *fast*. I thanked Elvis and walked back over and dropped into my seat. Shit. Could it be my old man wants these guys to beat me bad enough to shell out that kind of money for a Merlin Ultra-Lite? What the hell for?

Mr. Nak brought me back from a fantasy involving high explosives and my dad's pickup. "Let's wrap 'er up. I brought some grub from none of the basic food groups, and you're welcome to stay an' polish it off, or you can go commit whatever felonies and misdemeanors I've kept you from. Thanks for comin'. I hope you read some things tonight that will give you a differnt look at yourself."

It's a funny thing, Lar, Mr. Nak just *leaves* you with stuff. You want to ask him what to *do* with it, but you don't because he just tells you to do whatever your little cowboy heart desires, and leaves you frustrated. When you grow up in a world where adults delight in telling you what to do, then make your life miserable when you don't, Mr. Nak's style can be pretty unnerving, but in the long run I know it's best. A time is fast approaching when the universe will require me to make my own decisions and stand by them. But *damn*! When someone's as smart as Mr. Nak, you can't help but wish they'd give you a little push.

There was more to Valentine's night, Lar, but I'm getting serious drools and I can feel my eyelids about to slam shut. If you'll listen, you can hear them, too.

Whooosh! Bang! Bang! Bang! Bang! Bang! Bang! Bang!

Bo

"**W**hat did your valentine to Elvis say?" Bo asks as he and Shelly leave the Valentine's Day party and hurry down the walkway to the parking lot. The temperature has risen ever so slightly, and snowflakes drift lazily through the still air, dancing in the glow of the outdoor security lights.

"Who wants to know?"

"I wants to know."

"Why?"

"Just because of the way he looked at you," Bo says. "Whatever you wrote threw him off."

"I said I'd take care of his brothers and sisters."

"Seriously? You mean take them home?"

"Not for good, dummy. I just said I'd take them off his hands for a while sometimes. That would give him a chance to do things he needs to do without them. You know, get away from all the frustration of feeling like a failure, and getting so pissed."

"What are you going to do with them? I mean, these are Elvis's brothers and sisters. You think they're going to be like Care Bears or something?"

"Is your little brother a Care Bear?"

Bo is silent. The point is well taken.

"Haven't you figured it out, Bo?"

"Figured what out?"

"That there's something the same about every one of us in that group?"

"Well, yeah. I mean, we all screwed up some way to get there. We all have to get out of the group to get out of school."

Shelly shakes her head. "No. We all need to *stay*. We've all lost something, and only Mr. Nak and the people in the group know what it is. I understand that after tonight."

Bo stares blankly. He doesn't know what it is. At least he doesn't know the name for it.

Shelly seems to read his mind. "It's the truth," she says. "We lost the truth."

"What do you mean?"

They are near the Blazer, and Shelly swings her book bag off her shoulder, resting it on the sidewalk as she kneels to rummage through it. She removes a book. "Look at this," she says. "It's by a really smart woman named Alice Miller."

Bo stares at the cover: *For Their Own Good.* "I've heard that line a time or two."

"We all have. According to Alice Miller, it's used mostly when something isn't for our own good. Hey, I went to foster care for my own good, you spent nine months in your room for your own good, Hudge's dad burned his legs and killed his dog for his own good; it goes on and on."

Bo's eyes go soft as he stares above the Blazer at the snow falling through the glow of the streetlight. "My dad wants me to lose this triathlon for my own good. . . ."

"Exactly. So for starters, we've lost the truth. But we've also lost the people who took it from us. Elvis lost his dad, literally, I lost my family, Hudgie's lost . . . God, who knows what all Hudgie's lost. You've lost your dad—"

"I wish."

"No, don't you see? A real dad would never stack the deck against you. When he gives Wyrack's guys that bike, he's stealing the truth about how you really stack up against them—about who you are as an Ironman. Remember you told me once how you loved the way your dad used to teach you things—that he always let you learn how to *do* things on your own?"

"Yeah." For a reason he can't quite grasp, Bo feels a tightness in his throat. "Yeah," he says again.

"When was the last time you felt that?"

Bo smiles. "Long time."

"Don't you miss it?"

"Yeah, I miss it."

"That guy who taught you stuff, that was a dad. The guy who has to have his hand on the outcome of everything you do, the guy who's running around in the shadows doing his best to make sure you lose Yukon Jack's—he's no dad. Baby, you've lost him."

Bo takes Alice Miller's book from Shelly's hand, staring at the cover: *For Their Own Good.* "I can't believe I care."

Shelly places her hands on Bo's shoulders, stands on her tiptoes, and kisses his cheek. "But you do. And if you say you don't, you perpetuate the lie. That's why I told Elvis I'd take care of his brothers and sisters, because as ornery as he is, he's trying to do something different than his dad did. But *trying* to do something different doesn't get it. You have to *do* it. The only time I ever thought I saw that juvenile delinquent scared was when he thought he couldn't pull off taking care of those guys. Every time he hits his little brother, he carries on the family lie."

Bo considers his own rage, his stubbornness. It differs very little from his father's, or Elvis's for that matter. "So how do we fix this?" he says, still gazing at the book's cover. "Does Alice Miller tell us that?"

"Mr. Nak tells us that. Every day we sit in that group, he tells us that. About a week before you came, he said the most important thing he's ever said to me. He said, 'There is no act of heroism that doesn't include standing up for yourself.' *That's* how we fix it; we take back what we've lost. We give it to ourselves; we learn the truth, and we put it in place of the lie."

They step into the Blazer and snap the seat belts. "That has to be easier said than done," Bo says.

"No shit. And I think even when the lie is replaced, the scar remains. I could be the best, most famous American Gladiator ever, and I'd still miss the chance I should have had to be part of Redmond's basketball team—to get the varsity letter and the glory, and to suffer through the losses with my teammates. To belong. But what I lost makes me want what I want with *passion*. I'll be better for it, even though I'll hurt for it."

FEBRUARY 15 *Damned Early*

Dear Larry,

Awhile back, Mr. S. told me he didn't know where I'd find my Stotans, but to choose them carefully. Well, I know where they are now, Lar, though I'm not sure how to recruit them, and I've chosen them with the greatest of care.

A Stotan all the way,

Brewski

"**I**'m telling you, Shelly, these guys don't know they're sled dogs. My mother raises them because she likes the way they look, not because she longs to explore the Northern Slope."

"Don't worry about it. It's bred in," Shelly says back. "Besides, you've had them in harnesses a lot. It can't be much different dragging you down the road than pulling one of these." She points to the ancient sled she'd appropriated from a distant relative with a husky ranch in northern Idaho. The four younger dogs leap and scrap with one another, eager to go. "It's been cold; the snow down by the tracks should be packed hard. *This* will get you in shape."

"Yeah," Jordan says from his spot bundled up on the sled, "this will get you in shape."

"Yeah," mimics Fabian, Elvis's younger brother, from his position directly in front of Jordan, "get you in shape."

"Yeah," says Leslie, Elvis's four-year-old sister.

Bo glances around the yard, adjusting his ski mask. "Anybody else?"

"Yeah," Shelly says. "Get this right. You be the lead dog. I'll bet they'll go where you go. I figure they'll be too fast for the first mile or so, so I'll dig in and provide the drag. After that, you should be able to run right beside them, and I can ride with the Younger gang." She nods at the kids. "Now, mush! We're gonna get in some *miles*."

"Yeah," Jordan says. "Miles."

Bo crouches, placing his gloves on Jordan's cheeks. "Put a snowball in it, buddy, or I'll hang you out in front of these dogs like a carrot on a stick. And when we're through, I'll let 'em eat you."

"Heh!" Leslie says. "Eat you." She laughs like a maniac.

Jordan scoops a handful of snow and flips it in Bo's face.

An hour and fifteen minutes later, Bo sits in the deep snow of his backyard, gasping for air and nuzzling the dogs, adding them to his short list of Stotans. Inside, his mother and Shelly pour cups of hot chocolate for the kids and break up three two-fisted altercations between Fabian and Jordan, who has taken exception to Fabian's wholesale appropriation of his X-Men collection.

Ellen Brewster is mildly startled to find herself face-to-face with Elvis when she opens the door in response to the ringing of the bell. "Hi," she says, recovering quickly when she realizes who he is. "Come on in."

Elvis steps inside, removing his knitted cap. "I just come for my brother and sister."

"Would you like a cup of cocoa?" she asks, measuring him with her gaze. "Or coffee? A beer?"

Elvis smiles uneasily. "No, ma'am. I just come for the kids."

Bo is struck by Elvis's uneasiness. He seems uncomfortable there in the doorway, out of place in the surroundings of a comfortable home. And smaller. "Come on, man," he says. "Stay a few minutes, warm yourself up."

Elvis's jaw sets. "Nah, I just . . ."

Shelly is up, snatching Fabian's coat from the back of the couch. "Come on, you guys, your brother's here. Time to go."

Bo watches Elvis's face relax. He has something to learn about respecting a person's sphere of comfort.

"Hey, Ironman, you really think those things are going to help you?"

"I guess we'll see," Bo says back. Ian Wyrack has just finished ahead of him on eighteen of twenty hundred-yard sprints, and Bo's shoulders ache to the marrow.

Wyrack glances up at the pace clock, noting they have a minute before starting the next set. He reaches over the lane rope. "Lemme see those."

Bo slips the rubberized webbed gloves off his hands, passing them across. Wyrack measures their weight in his hand, then slips one on. "Heavy," he says. He turns his hands over and back, assessing the gloves. "Where'd you get these?"

"My girlfriend got them out of a Speedo catalog."

"The dyke comes through."

Bo has long since learned not to take the bait. "The dyke comes through," he says back.

Wyrack removes the gloves. "You really think these are going to make a difference?"

"Hey," Bo says, "the first day I had 'em, you beat me on every repeat. Today I got two. Tomorrow it'll be three."

"You dipshit. I'm starting to taper for Nationals. You beat me because I backed off."

Bo smiles and retrieves the glove, directing his nod upward. "The clock says different."

Wyrack finishes ahead of Bo by a body length on nine of the next ten in a set of two hundreds, but Bo touches him out on the last. The ache in his arms and shoulders deepens in response to the extra pound inserted inside the back of each glove and the resistance of the webs. He glances at the clock: nearly a full second under Wyrack's time standard. "Tapering?" he gasps.

"Up yours," Wyrack gasps back.

"Tomorrow I'll get two."

"Get me on as many as you want. This'll all be settled at Yukon Jack's."

"That it will," Bo says. "Tell you how I got it figured. You been bustin' your butt in this pool since September. You'll go to Nationals in two weeks, and probably do okay, come back here to a ticker-tape parade and have to start training all over again—while your buddies are hitting the keggers and leading the good life. Sun'll come out and the guys'll head for the beach, but you'll be stuck here swimming back and forth, back and forth, staring at that ugly black line when you should be out testing the back roads in that hot car of yours. And what for? Just to prove you and two other guys can take a skinny punk high schooler to the cleaners. Could be hard to keep up the motivation, Wyrack, know what I mean?"

"You're forgetting something," Wyrack says. "I'll be relieving the skinny punk high schooler's dyke girlfriend of five hundred green ones, most of which she'll probably have to get from him unless she wants to spend some serious hours on her back. And besides, Ironman, the key to our success lies with our biker. You'll never get close enough to *see* me in the water. I'll be dried off and out testing the back roads while you're sprinting for the finish line."

"We'll see."

"Yes, we will."

"Mr. Brewster, could I see you for a moment?"

Bo stops in the doorway to the hall. "Sure," he says, and steps aside to let the rest of the Senior English students pass. He walks slowly back to Redmond's desk and waits.

"Are you aware that you are no longer required to attend Mr. Nakatani's anger management group?"

"Yeah."

"Well, I'm aware that you're still attending."

"Yeah."

"I'm saying you can call it good," Redmond says. "I think it's time you got on with things."

Bo nods.

"Good, then. I'll write a note to Mr. Nakatani, and you can end your participation as of today."

Bo nods again.

"Mr. Brewster," Redmond says at the sound of the bell ending class, "could I see you for a moment?"

Bo waits again in the doorway for the rest of the class to pass into the hall, then moves back toward Redmond's desk.

"I thought I told you last week that you could end your participation in Mr. Nakatani's anger management group."

"Yes sir. You did."

"I'm told you're still attending."

"Yes sir. I am."

"I don't understand."

Bo raises his eyebrows and shrugs.

Redmond bristles. "Are you playing stupid with me, young man?"

"No sir."

"There are students in greater need of Mr. Nakatani's group than yourself, Mr. Brewster. I'd appreciate it if you would withdraw."

"Mr. Nakatani told me there was plenty of room," Bo says. "I told him I'd pull out if he needed the space, but he said it was up to me." He is careful to display no disrespect, show no emotion. Mr. Nak's anger management techniques are indeed paying off.

"Well, as the teacher who directed you to that group," Redmond says, "I am now directing you out of that group. Do you understand?"

"Yes sir."

"Mr. Brewster. See me after class," Mr. Redmond says as his Senior English class files into the room.

"Mr. Brewster," Redmond says fifty-five minutes later, when the students are gone, "I directed you to cease participation in Mr. Nakatani's anger management group last week. You told me you would do that."

"No sir, I didn't. You asked me if I understood, and I said I did. I didn't say I'd quit the group."

Redmond leans forward onto his elbows. "You know something, Brewster? I'm about up to here with your attitude. You've done a good job in here since your last blowup, and I've treated you with respect in response to that. But you need to learn to follow directions. Now, if you'd like me to take this to a higher authority, I'll be glad to do that, but I would rather settle it between the two of us."

Bo drops his book into his book bag, slings it over his shoulder, and says, "I vote for a higher authority."

FEBRUARY 26

Dear Larry,

Are you ever embarrassed to be an adult just because of the way other adults act? That happens to me sometimes with teenagers. The TV news will report a kid blowing somebody away at school, or raping a retarded girl, or committing some equally unspeakable act, and his attorney will use the fact that he's a kid to get him tried as a juvenile where nothing much can happen to him. Then I wonder how the fact that someone hasn't been on the planet quite eighteen years relieves him of responsibility for the horror his actions bring upon his victims and their families. I don't know the answer to the question, but I know I feel a sense of shame when I think society could excuse me for committing some atrocity because I'm seventeen years old.

Anyway, the reason I brought it up is that Mr. Redmond is seeming more and more like a cartoon character to me, and rather than getting angry at him, I'm starting to get embarrassed for him.

It has taken a long time for me to understand Mr. Nak's notion that my anger is a cover for my fear, and only when I admit to that fear will I get control of my anger, or in fact have no need for it. I am coming to understand that the fear comes from feeling inadequate when Redmond or my dad pushes me, and if I can acknowledge it, there's no need to cover it. Believe me, Lar, that's a lot easier said than done, because it's a natural, unthinking thing to haul out your rage in a flash so no one sees how scared you are. But understanding that—truly *understanding* it—is like being handed a secret of the universe, because people look different to me then: my dad, Redmond, even guys like Elvis.

Mr. Nak taught me a trick. He told me to think of fear

as a *person* who's going to be around whether he's invited or not. He said, "Think of him like a big ol' bully pain-in-the-butt cousin you cain't get rid of, an' the only way to get your binniss done is to allow him to tag along, because he's goin' to anyway. Then don't take your eye off him a minute, so he don't get the chance to make you look like a horse's patoot."

So I took my big ol' bully pain-in-the-butt cousin in with me to talk to Redmond, and guess what? It works! I'm standing there in front of him three separate times while he tries to get me to quit Mr. Nak's group. First he suggests it, then he pushes it, then he demands it. Now as much as I sound like a smartass when I talk about him, he scares me. There's no other way to say it: *He scares me.* I told Mr. Nak that earlier, and this is how he helped me out. He said, "So what is it exactly you're scared of, Bo?" I said I'm scared of *Redmond*, and he says, "But what can he do? He cain't send you to Anger Management; he already done that. He cain't hurt you bodily because of the law. He cain't say bad things to your dad, because he's already said 'em. He cain't throw you off the football team, because you're done throwed off. Hell, that man's done his worst damage already, an' you're still standin'. What's scarin' ya?"

I said, "I'm not sure. . . ."

"Well, maybe it's not him you're afraid of. Who else is there?"

"Me? Myself?"

"That'd be a guess worth lookin' at," he said with a smile. "So what is it about you you're afraid of?"

"God, I don't know."

"Don't quit on me here." Mr. Nak's eyes narrowed. "What is it about you you're afraid of?"

"I don't know. I mean, it's the way I *feel*. It's—"

"Bingo!" he says before I can finish. "B-six and goddamn bingo! You're afraid of how you feel. *That's* the fear inside I been talkin' about. It's gonna be there because it's about you, not Mr. Redmond. An' it'll be there for the next guy who acts like Mr. Redmond an' the guy after that. Know why that is?"

I shook my head.

"Who does Mr. Redmond act like?"

I nodded. "He acts like my dad."

"Okay. An' when your dad looks down on you, or cuts you, or lashes you with words . . .''

"I hate it."

"That the feelin' you're afraid of?"

I nodded. I felt beaten. It reminded me of second grade when our teacher said each of us had a skeleton inside us; you know, to hold up your body. I'd been watching some horror flick with witches and werewolves and skeletons and stuff, and it absolutely terrorized me, Lar, because I couldn't figure out how I was going to get away from a monster that lived *inside* me.

But Mr. Nak kept at it. "So you have the answer. It ain't about Redmond, it's about you. When you come face-to-face with this here Jesse James of a football coach, you tell your pain-in-the-butt cousin, Fear, he can come along if he wants to, but you're gonna take care of binniss once an' for all, no matter what he does or says, because you're by God fed up with gettin' jerked around. His presence ain't gonna change your actions one whit."

We were in group when he said this, and every person who was willing to speak up knew of a fear of their own just like mine. Shuja refused to call it that—he called it "rattly nerves"—but it was the same.

So like I started to tell you, Lar, I hung back each time Redmond said he wanted to talk to me after class, and I just nodded and said I knew I could leave Anger Management anytime and refused to give a reason why I wouldn't. I watched the temperature rise behind his eyes and counted the heartbeats in his temple and kept on shinin' on. And you know what? Pain-in-the-butt Cousin Fear must have gotten bored, because when I looked up to walk out of the room, he was nowhere to be found, and I was feeling *big*.

I don't know exactly what Redmond's agenda with me is, Lar. I don't think I could have made a difference in the football team's win-loss record this year, and I can't imagine that he cares what I think of him. But he does have an agenda and I better not forget it, because I've gotten under his skin, and he feels good when I feel bad. Plus, I've heard my dad's words coming out of his mouth, and vice versa, far more times than coincidence would allow, so I best keep in mind that they're in cahoots. I've looked carefully at the damage he can do, and it's not much, really; Mr. Nak was right. I have copies of all my assignments and test scores, so he can't flunk me in English. When I know, you'll know.

> Tower of Power,
>
> Bo

Bo finishes cleaning the offices at the newspaper early and jogs down Main Street, hoping to catch his father before the store closes. It has been weeks since Elvis delivered the information about the freebie special-order bike supposedly destined for Wyrack's relay team, and he has avoided bringing it up, partly because he doesn't want to believe it and partly because he does believe it and can't find words for the confrontation.

He stands outside Brewster's Sporting Goods, waiting for the last customer to leave. As Curt, the salesman, moves toward the door to lock it, he steps in.

"Hey, Bo, how you doin'?"

"Doin' good. My dad around?"

Curt points to the rear of the store. "In his office."

"He alone?"

"I think so. Mr. Redmond, you guy's football coach, was back there with him earlier, but I think I saw him leave about fifteen minutes ago. Hey, how's the training going? Heard you're getting serious about Yukon Jack's this year."

Bo smiles. "Goin' good. Yeah, pretty serious." It's difficult for Bo to discern what's been said about him around the store, whether Curt is playing dumb or whether his father is keeping his plans to himself. He decides to play it as it lays. "Hey, Curt, you know a guy named Lonnie Gerback? A swimmer from CFU? And a cyclist?"

"Yeah, I know him," Curt says. "Tall guy, sandy hair. Got some thighs on 'im."

"That's him," Bo says. "He do business here?"

"Yeah, that's how I know him. In fact we ordered him a monster racer; one of those Merlin Ultra-Lites like you were trying to deal with your dad for. Kid must be a serious racer. Must have some bucks, too. That sweet thing runs about five grand."

Thanks, Curt. That's what I wanted to know.

"Think Dad could get a better deal if he ordered two?" Bo asks jokingly.

Curt laughs, and Bo follows the aisle toward his father's office.

"Tell your dad I'm outta here," Curt hollers after him, and Bo raises a hand to indicate he heard.

Bo pulls the office door shut behind him. "Hey, Dad."

Lucas looks up from the paperwork on his desk, removing his glasses. "Hey, son. How are you?"

"Fine," Bo says. "Just got off and thought I'd stop and say hi."

"Caught me trying to catch up," Lucas says, pushing the papers to the side, "but I'm never caught up anyway. Want to grab some dinner?"

"You buyin'?"

"I'm buyin' mine," Lucas says.

"Sad to say, that's the best offer I've had all day." Bo stands, glimpsing the half-hidden order form for the Ultra-Lite he believes his father is bankrolling for Lonnie Gerback. (His ability to read upside down has served him well in the past when he needed to snag a test answer from a teacher's guide lying open on the teacher's desk.) He catches NIE GERB and some measurements. "Somebody buying a Merlin?" he asks, giving away nothing of his suspicions.

"Yeah," his father says. "A young kid up at the university. A pretty good cyclist, I understand."

"Must be a *hell* of a cyclist, or at least think he is. That's an expensive bike."

"That it is. I understand his parents are quite wealthy."

Bo reaches across and picks up the Merlin ad from the top of the pile. "Man, you know how I'd like to get my hands on one of these."

"Salt a couple more thousand away, and it's yours," Lucas says. "A piece of machinery like this has to be earned."

Bo smiles. "Yeah, I guess so. No chance of somebody just plopping one of these babies in your lap."

"No, I wouldn't think so," Lucas says.

MARCH 3

Dear Larry,

Hey, Lar, it's getting close. Wyrack and the rest of the CFU team go to NAIA Nationals at the end of this week, and Yukon Jack's is exactly six weeks from the day they get back. I won't have the CFU team to push me anymore, so I'll have to learn to push myself. I can't back off now. They've been tapering in practice, but Mr. S has altered my workout so I get in extra laps during their rest periods. And I think the webbed hand weights are helping. When I take them off, I feel propeller-driven. Mr. S also said he'd take me out to Williams Lake as soon as the ice is off, to get in some good open-water distance. I'm grateful, but I gotta tell you, Williams Lake is *cold* this time of year. I have no idea whether I can take these guys, I really don't, but I'll tell you what: They're gonna by God know they've been in a race, because I'm pissed.

My dad is lying to me straight out. I had dinner with him the other night and gave him every opportunity to tell me about the bike he's fronting for Wyrack's biker, but he acted like he couldn't even remember the kid's name. I know he swore those guys to secrecy, and he'll probably even write up paperwork to make it look like a righteous sale. Then when I confront him, he'll say he did it so I wouldn't get too big for my britches. He'll say he did it for my own good, to let me know how tough the world is. And he's gonna hear from me then, Lar, because having your old man line up with a stranger behind your back is not for your own good, and he'd better hire Abraham Lincoln to deliver *that* address if he wants me to believe it.

See, I blasted awake out of a dream the same night I had dinner with him, and though I couldn't remember what I'd dreamed, I was sweating like a pig, and in a big-time rage, and it was a Lucas Brewster dream for sure. I knew I wouldn't get any more sleep, because there's only one way to blow one of those out of your system, and that's with *vigorous* exercise, so I pulled on two sets of sweats and my running shoes and hit the two A.M. streets. I've said before that the rhythm of my feet on the road frees my mind, but I couldn't get it loose. All I could see was my dad sitting across the table being relatively nice to me (he actually did pick up the tab for dinner) and even asking about my training—at the same time he was trying to sabotage my big moment. And all I could do was hate him.

Approximately eight miles and an hour later, I found myself cruising by Mr. S's place, and though it was really late (or really early, depending on your perspective), a light shone in his living-room window, and I took a chance that it was Mr. S and not his roommate. Hey, if there's anyone in the world to ask about dads, Lar, it has to be Mr. S, who struggles daily to come to terms with a father who will never answer even one question.

"There's no answer to this," Mr. S said, after I told him why I was logging training miles at a time of night when only vampires and werewolves should be on the streets. I'd been lucky; caught him pulling an all-nighter making lesson plans for his sub for the week he's at Nationals with the university team. "I think it doesn't help you to try to make sense of your dad's motives. I mean, you guys are locked in a power struggle, and nothing is going to make sense until one of you releases."

I said, "I suppose it has to be me, right? God, Mr. S, how can I do that?"

"You probably can't," he said. "You're probably going to play it out."

"So what would you do if you were me?"

"If I were *you*," he said, "I'd probably run marathons in the middle of the night and push weights until my arms fell off and tie a bowling ball around my waist to swim the English Channel. If I were *me* in your position, I'd focus on my goal, train hard but sensibly, and tell myself twelve times a day that it's not helping me to let my behavior match my inner craziness, or to let my outer craziness match my father's."

"So what would you do if you were you in my position, but also my age?"

"I'd do the same thing you're doing," he said. "But it wouldn't help me." He leaned forward. "Listen, Bo, you and your dad aren't going to iron out your differences in this triathlon. This triathlon is about you, not him. This is *your* challenge. If you let him take it away from you, you'll hate him—and yourself—even more. Now go home and go to bed."

I gotta tell you, Lar, if there's a heaven, and I lead a decent enough life from here on in to get a shot at entry, my challenge will be explaining how I ever turned my back on that guy.

> Ever forward,
>
> The Midnight Racer

CHAPTER 14

"I think I got us a project," Shuja says to start the anger management session.

"An' what kinda project would that be, Mr. Shu?" Nak says.

"This a filthy project."

Nak shakes his head. "Seems like we got enough hard times around here without takin' on somethin' filthy."

Shuja laughs, remembering to whom he is speaking. "Filthy mean *good* to you, Mr. Nak. It's a *good* project."

"In that case, I'm chompin' at the bit."

Shu glances at the faces in the circle. "I think we gotta get behind the Ironman."

Faces stare blankly.

"See," Shuja continues, "way I see it, Rock 'n' Roll right about Ironman. He different from us, but not for the reason Rock 'n' Roll think. Ironman different 'cause he can *do* somethin' about what ails him."

Nak says, "Interestin' thought. Keep talkin'."

"Well," Shuja says, nodding toward Hudgie, present for the first time since his hospitalization, "take Hudge here. Cain't do *nothin'* 'bout what's goin' on in his life but get some miles between him an' it. Rock 'n' Roll stuck takin' care of his family: Daddy's split, little brother and sister hammerin' at him all the time, got a full-time job keepin' his head above water. Wonder Woman done los' her childhood, if you wanna know. Got it robbed right from her. All kinda different foster parents an' shit; John Wayne Redmond cheatin' her outta her rightful high-school glory, an' who knows what all else. Resta these guys, who knows what boogeymen after them, they never speak up. Me, I got all of history to take on; no way I can fix that 'fore the end-of-the-year picnic."

Shuja nods toward Bo, who listens intently. "But Ironman, he know the enemy. He got Tweedledumb an' Tweedledumber for a daddy an' a coach, an' a buncha smartass college boys with a bad attitude an' a rocket bicycle his own daddy give 'em to help 'em kick his boy's ass. I think it might help this group manage a whole buncha anger to see at least *one* enemy get—" and he pushes his thumb hard against his knee, as if squashing a bug.

"Whaddaya want us to do?" Elvis says. "Start runnin' an' ridin' our bikes an' headin' for the old swimmin' hole with our buddy Bo?"

"Don' worry, Rock 'n' Roll, this won't require much BTU output by you. I'm talkin' support team here."

"Support team?" Elvis says. "Whaddaya mean, support team? Hey, man, I ain't gonna be nobody's ni—"

"Nigger?" Shuja says with a smile. "Hey, say it, man. I can respect a man who shows hisself. Besides, the day *you* somebody's nigger'll be the best day of your life. Now, here's what I think. . . ."

MARCH 23

Dear Larry,

Sorry I haven't kept up, Lar, but it's a little more than a month until Yukon Jack's, and there's been almost no time for anything but training, sleep, and schoolwork, where I'm hanging in at a low C in most of my classes, with the exception of English, where I have about ten points more than I need for an A plus. I figure I'll need that to pull a D out of Redmond. Yukon Jack's is taking on greater and greater significance as zero hour draws nearer, which is both scary and exciting. Some kids in the Home Ec. class made me a jersey with my name and CLARK FORK BLACKHAWKS on the back, and a picture of a stiff eagle stuck beakfirst into the ground on the front. The CFU mascot is an eagle. Rumor has it Redmond attempted to get any school recognition of my performance officially blocked, because it could provide fertile ground for my kind of moral attitude to grow. Rumor also has it that Dr. Stevens told him to grow up and get with the program. If that conversation actually took place, I would offer up a small, round vital organ lodged very close to my left leg to have been witness to it.

Wyrack's team is training full bore these days, but I think I may have been right when I said he'd have a hard time getting back into it after Nationals. He didn't get back into the water for at least a week and a half after they returned, and he had already cut his workout distances in half tapering for that meet. I haven't worked out at the CFU pool when he's around. Good as I'm feeling, he still intimidates me, and if he's getting back into peak condition, I don't want to know it. I see Gerback hammering out miles on the road now and then, and I don't like what I see. Man, I don't know why my dad thinks he needs the Ultra-Lite. The bike he's got now is turbocharged, and the guy's got thighs like oil drums. And Gerback's got the passion; he's a serious racer.

I finally found out who their runner is, and that's the good news. His name is Kenny Joseph. Pretty good individual medley man—placed in the consolation finals at Nationals—but swimmers are notoriously slow on land, so I doubt he's some web-footed Herb Elliot. Shelly saw him working out at the university track a few days ago, and she said there was no smoke coming out of the cinders behind him. So Yukon Jack McCoy's biases are turning out in my favor. Cyclists go first, so all the damage will be done in the beginning. However much distance Gerback gets on me will be what I have to make up in the run and the swim.

I start swimming in Williams Lake tomorrow. Mr. S is going to pace me in a rowboat. Hey, Lar, remember that vital organ I said I'd be willing to donate to witness Dr. Stevens telling Redmond what for? Well, it won't be worth much after I hit the water tomorrow, because I'll be lucky if it doesn't freeze harder than a marble and drop to the bottom of Williams Lake. That water's *cold*.

My Stotans are in place, Lar, and I didn't have to recruit them. I showed up at the weight room the other day, and who was there but Shuja, decked out in baggy shorts and a tank top, with more muscles than I have places, ready to push me through the workout. It's not like it took all that much for him—hell, he could lift me while I'm lifting weights—but he ran me through all the machines, then pushed me through some free weights, joking about whether I was going to write home on those pencils I have for arms. I probably put in half again my usual workout.

Then I'm biking over the back roads toward Spangle, and Elvis pulls up beside me in his old man's pickup, paces me for almost twenty miles. Hudgie's in the back, holding up a handmade sign that says KICK BUTT FOR ANGRY MANAGEMENT. Mr. Nak said anyone who participates in this madness need come to group only once a week, so I've got guys I barely know driving up beside me in the middle of eastern Washington scabland, handing me Gatorade and peeling me bananas. It's hard to say how good it feels to have these lunatics behind me, and harder to say how scared I am to let them down.

I finally told Mom about Dad buying the Ultra-Lite for Gerback, and I truly believed she would storm down to the store, pop out his eyeballs, and eat 'em like grapes, she was so mad, but I convinced her to let it ride. When I face him down on this one, I want to take him by surprise.

That bike is going to cost me some valuable time. The titanium frame weighs about the same as a kite, and the entire machine has less than zero wind resistance. Tell you what, if it were up to me, we'd all ride on 1955 balloon-tire Schwinns. That would separate the men from the goddamn astronauts.

From this point on, Lar, all I can do is train and race. Since that doesn't make real good copy, my next contact with you will be from the victory stand.

Your man of steel in the Northwest,

Clark Kent

"The name's Na—"

"I know who you are, Mr. Nakatani. What can I do for you?" Lucas Brewster stands behind the checkout counter just inside the entrance to Brewster's Sporting Goods, absently running a dust rag over the till.

"Thought we might have a word about your boy."

"Is he bombing out of Anger Management, too?" Luke asks.

Nak straddles a weight bench placed in front of a free-weight display next to the door. "Nope, he sure ain't. He's doin' real fine in Anger Management, as a matter of fact."

"So what's the problem?"

"I didn't say there was a problem," Nak says. "I just thought we might have a word about him. About him and you, actually."

"Of course," Lucas says. "I can take time where my boys are concerned."

"That's good to know. Can't say the same for the parents of all the kids I work with."

"I imagine not," Lucas says. "So tell me why you've come."

"I've come because I believe a lot of the boy's problems could be resolved by working on his relationship with you."

"You're saying Bo's problems are my fault?"

Nak smiles and shakes his head. "Not at all. I'm sayin' I believe a lot of his problems could be resolved by workin' on his relationship with you. The way a boy is with his father means a lot."

Lucas stares at his desk. "Well, Mr. Nakatani, my boy doesn't seem to see it that way."

"That's because he's a boy, Mr. Brewster. It seems to me that the two of you are locked in a power struggle that's tearin' the both of you up."

"That's not a power struggle of my making. Bo knows what he has to do to meet my standards."

"To my mind," Naks says, "don't much matter who's makin' the struggle, only that it's there. One side or t'other has to ease up."

"I've tried everything I could think of with that boy, Mr. Nakatani, and nothing works."

"I'm assumin' you're aware of this Yukon Jack's thing he's out there killin' himself for."

"Oh, yes," Lucas says, "I'm aware of it."

"It's real important to him, sir. I'm thinkin' it might be a place to start mendin' some fences. It'd change his whole picture of things if he had your support."

Lucas leans back against the counter, folding his arms. "I'm afraid I can't do that. If I have anything to say about it, Bo's going to learn an important lesson on that day."

"An' what lesson would that be?"

"He's going to learn the cost of having things his own way. And he's going to learn about quitters."

Nak smiles again. "Oh, Mr. Brewster, I don't think he'll quit."

"He already did," Lucas says, his eyes narrowing. "Let's stop playing games, Mr. Nakatani. You know Bo quit the football team this year. In fact, I'll bet you know a lot about Bo, and you most likely know a lot about me, or at least Bo's perception of me."

"I know some of his perceptions."

"So you must think I'm a pretty unreasonable man."

"I ain't had a lot of reason to judge. I've perty much been focused on your boy."

"Well, let me tell you something," Lucas says, as if he hadn't heard Nak's last sentence. "I'm not unreasonable at all. I'm sure I made some mistakes with Bo—no parent is perfect—but

I don't need some self-righteous Zen-thinking outsider to give me advice about my relationship with my son. I've put some feelers out, Mr. Nakatani, and I have a pretty good idea what goes on in that so-called anger management group of yours. In fact, I've been thinking of bringing it up with school authorities, because I don't think you're helping those kids, entertaining their juvenile ideas—"

Nak holds up his hands. "Whoa, whoa. Rein 'er in there a minute. I didn't realize I was in hostile territory. I thought we were talking about your son."

"Mr. Nakatani, do you have children?"

Nak's eyes soften, and he leans back on the bench. "Is that important?"

"It is to me, because I think you may be meddling in something you don't understand. Do you have children, Mr. Nakatani."

"No sir, not anymore."

"Not anymore. Then I take it you're divorced?"

"My children are dead, Mr. Brewster."

Nak's frankness stuns Lucas, and he sits back. "Oh, I'm sorry. . . ."

"Two daughters an' a son. Killed in a car wreck, back in Texas."

"I really am sorry to hear that. I just—"

"They died 'cause I was drivin' drunk."

Lucas stares.

"Right around Christmastime," Nak says. "Three kids, all under the age of six. Went to a party at a parent's house; got to drinkin' this here special homemade eggnog, had a powerful bunch of rum in it. I dropped my wife home around midnight— my ex-wife now—an' drove over to the baby-sitter's to round up the kids. Crazy thing, the night started off almost seventy degrees. Time I picked up the kids, we were in the middle of one of them hard-blowin' west Texas ice storms. I'm three sheets to the wind bringin' 'em home anyway, an' the damn wipers just keep blurrin' the ice across the windshield. Happened real simple-like; quick, too. See these headlights comin' around the canyon bend an' I tap the brakes, tryin' to pull to the shoulder an' stop because I can't see. Next thing I know, I'm slidin' broadside an' them headlights are growin' like the devil's eyes."

Nak stands, looking shaken. "Not a scratch on me, Mr. Brewster. Not a scratch. Car's flat on the shotgun side where my boy is, an' the entire backseat is gone. Driver's side is untouched." Nak takes a deep breath. "Universe made a bubble for me, Mr. Brewster. I was untouched, an' my children are dead." Nak pulls on his jacket. "Well, I tell you what sir. I sobered up right quick. I can't tell you all I wished."

Lucas is silent, his eyes averted from Nak's steely gaze.

"So no, Mr. Brewster, I don't have children. But I know about 'em. I figure I know just about how precious they are; I think I know that, sir. An' I think I know about missed opportunities."

Lucas regains his composure. "I'm sorry about your family, Mr. Nakatani. I truly am. But wouldn't you say it's possible you have an agenda now, when you work with these kids?"

"An agenda? No sir, I wouldn't say I have an agenda. I'd call it more like a crusade." He thinks a moment. "Yeah, I'd call it a crusade."

"So you figure you can pay for your sins working with other people's children. That's admirable, but . . ."

Nak's smile is humorless. "You don't pay for that kind of sin, sir. You beg the universe to teach you the quality of mercy, is what you do, so you can get from one day to the next. An' then you stand up for kids ever time you get the chance, an' you stand up for their parents, too, because I'll tell you what: I can't stand up for your boy without standing up for you. This is about a father's relationship with his son, an' it's either gonna be there for the both of you, or neither."

Lucas takes a deep breath. He is touched by the intensity of this man, and he is touched by his story, But he thinks that this strange Asian cowboy clearly has no sense of what a father-son relationship truly is; how tightly the band between the two needs to be stretched so that the son does not take over. "Mr. Nakatani, I admire what you're trying to do, I really do. But I'm already working with someone from your school on my son's problems, and I'm afraid it's someone who shares a philosophy closer to mine."

Nak leans forward on the counter, his body weight supported almost entirely by the iron strands of his arms. "At the risk of wearin' out a welcome I never had," he says quietly, "I'm not talkin' about you workin' on your son's problems. That's the boy's job. An' like I said, he ain't doin' bad. I'm talkin' about settin' the stage for how the two of you will be with each other for the rest of your lives." He relaxes a bit and sighs. "Your son's seventeen, Mr. Brewster. His problems belong to him now."

A cold cloud settles in over Lucas Brewster. He has been told to let his son find his own way in the world one time too many. "You're right about one thing, Mr. Nakatani. You're about to wear out your welcome. Now, I don't believe in coddling kids, and you do. We're not going to agree on that, so let's just stop talking about it. Bo has been a rebel all his life, and if he doesn't get it under control he's going to be miserable for the rest of it. I don't have a lot of control over what happens to him, because he doesn't live with me, and he won't listen anyway. But any chance I get to influence things from behind the scenes, I'll do that. I'm not saying I *am* doing that, but I will at any opportunity. Now, you're a professional and so am I. I'm trusting that this conversation will not go back to my son. When I want him to have information, I'll give it to him. I don't want you meddling in my life, Mr. Nakatani, so do we have that agreement?"

Nak straightens to leave. "Yes sir, we do have that agreement. Your son doesn't need me to interpret what's goin' on between y'all. I won't involve myself in your life, like you asked. But let me tell you somethin'. I'm an adult, an' your son's a child.

In a good tribe every adult is a parent to every child, so don't ask me to take myself out of Bo's life as well."

When the door closes and Lucas is alone in the office, rage nearly consumes him. He has a mind to show up at the principal's office tomorrow morning and demand that Mr. Nakatani do his job and cease meddling in people's lives. He will not take advice from a man who admittedly screwed up his own family's life with alcohol, then decided to take a hand in Lucas Brewster's. And he is damned sick and tired of all these bleeding hearts taking up for Bo just because the boy throws out a little charm.

I went too far, Nak thinks, walking down the sidewalk outside Brewster's Sporting Goods. I gave him information he couldn't use, an' I scared him. I should have let it be. It's gonna play out whether I like it or not. An' I guess it needs to.

CHAPTER 15

Bo packs his gear carefully into the back of the Blazer late Friday afternoon. Yukon Jack's River Resort lies eighty-five miles south and west of Clark Fork, and he'll drive halfway this evening, then camp along the river. His mother and Jordan will drive down early tomorrow morning with Lionel and Mr. Nakatani, leading the Angry Management Caravan, as Hudgie calls it.

Tonight Bo wants to be alone with his challenge. When your role in life is to be a smartass for the benefit of all within earshot, he tells himself, it's good to get alone and welcome some seriousness. Yukon Jack's is famous throughout the state for its carnival atmosphere, and many physically less-taxing events than the triathlon are scheduled for this weekend: contests for beer guzzling, sailing cow pies, chasing tumbleweeds, and the like. There is need for focus.

He drives under the speed limit to a wide, calm spot on the river where his father used to take him fishing, and he sets up a small camp only feet from the shoreline. Wrapped in a warm jacket and watching the sun drop below the bluffs across the river, he considers the sadness lodged like an anvil in his chest. At five, he caught his first fish in this exact spot. Lucas Brewster patiently showed him how to bait his hook, helped him cast his line into the smooth, flowing waters. He untangled Bo's line from the reeds growing close to shore eight or nine times before the tiny fish finally struck, and he stood back and let the boy bring it in alone. Bo felt so proud he thought his chest would burst.

Where was that father? What happened to him? How did it get like this?

Sitting on the shore now, watching the last light give way to a moonless night so dark the sky seems a carpet of stars, Bo looks to his future. He'll graduate in less than a month, maybe go to college next year, maybe get a job. A lot depends on Shelly's plans, because he can't imagine not having her there to touch. Whatever he chooses, he promises himself, he'll always give himself physical challenges. He loves the way his body has responded over these past months as he stretched, tuned, and pushed it toward Yukon Jack's, hugely thankful for the way it has encased his spirit and his mind.

As he drifts into dreamless sleep, the air crisp inside his nostrils, crickets singing, stars dancing, Bo Brewster yearns to become a man.

"Got you some headgear," Shuja says, handing Bo a light blue sailor's hat, brim turned down all around. A set of Sportsman earphones is hemmed into the underside, the cord dangling down the back. STOTAN is embroidered in rainbow colors across the front. "Keep the sun offa you head in the run," Shuja says. "Fit under your helmet on the bike." He hands Bo a neoprene belt and pouch with a Walkman inside. "Words of wisdom in there," Shuja says. "Punch 'em at the gun."

Bo turns the hat over in his hands, then tries it on. The 'phones are perfectly placed, and the cord is just long enough to reach the tune belt when he straps it around his waist. He pops open the Walkman to see a tape with a blank label, smiles, and shakes his head, imagining what wisdom must lie within.

The parking lot at Yukon Jack's boat landing, on the shore of the Columbia River near the southern border of the state, is beginning to fill with cars, many outfitted with bicycle racks supporting the latest in sleek, colorful, technologically advanced two-wheel rockets, and vans with license-plate holders reading TRIATHLETES DO IT IN THREES and MARATHON MAN and such. Flashy rainbow cycle wear stretches tight over four percent body fat as contestants perform last-minute fine-tuning on spokes and sprockets, and joke with familiar faces.

Bo opens the back of the Blazer, glancing around in search

of the CFU team as he carefully removes his racer. He examines the interior of the bicycle seat bag for his extra tube and repair equipment, then checks the cooler for Gatorade, which he will dump into his drinking bottle shortly before the race starts.

"Great hat," Shelly says, moving toward him from the late registration table.

"Like that? Shuja gave it to me a minute ago. It's a regular mobile sound system. He said there are words of wisdom on this tape. Wanna check it out?"

"Touch the play button before the gun goes off, and I tear off your arms," Shelly says. "That tape is perfectly timed."

Bo pulls his air pump from the back of the Blazer, shaking his head and smiling. They made me a tape, he thinks. Is that great or what?

Muffled rock pulsates across the dusty parking lot as Ian Wyrack pulls in, seat-dancing to a bass-heavy version of "Fire Lake." He cuts the engine but remains in the car until the song is finished, glancing out at Bo. He gives a quick wave that turns into an extended middle finger the moment Bo waves back.

"He's a real prick, isn't he?" The voice comes from behind.

"That doesn't give pricks much credit," Bo says, and turns, discovering himself face-to-face with Lonnie Gerback. "Hey, Lonnie, how ya doin'? Think you can give these guys a big enough lead?"

"Gonna try," Lonnie says. "Cycling season starts pretty soon, and I want to hammer out a short one to see where I am."

It does not bode well for Bo Brewster that Lonnie Gerback considers this race a "short one," but his respect does not register. He nods at the sleek black racer beside Gerback. "Nice bike."

"Hell of a nice bike," Lonnie says. "Want to try it?"

"What?"

"This bike. You want to try it out?"

Bo shakes his head. "It'll just make me jealous for the race."

"No, I mean *use* it in the race."

Bo stares at the bike a moment. It is a flawless piece of technology. "What's the catch?"

Lonnie smiles. "The catch is, I'll beat you anyway. I'm a racer, man. I don't need space-age technology to run down a plodder. That's what I consider you multisport guys. I'm a purist."

"You're serious?" Bo says. "You'd let me ride this?"

"Wouldn't have it any other way."

Bo stares again at the bike, not knowing how to feel.

Lonnie slides his index finger under the crossbar and lifts the bike off the ground. "Defies gravity."

"Why you doin' this, man?"

"Truth?"

"Truth."

"Two reasons. One, you gave me a good push through the swimming season. While you were over there battling it out with Wyrack, I was using you as a standard for my own times. I'm not as fast on repeats as either of you guys, but I never back off. I like that about you, too, Ironman; you never back off. Gave me something to shoot for. When you weren't there, Wyrack was so inconsistent I'd even beat him on two or three. Hell, I picked up a couple of consolation bracket wins at Nationals because of you."

"That right? Cool. What's the other reason?"

"My old man."

"Oh, yeah? What about him?"

"Well, first he asked whether I was sure I wanted to be part of whatever war you were having with your dad."

"Did you tell him what that war was?"

"I've never met your dad," Lonnie says. "He and Wyrack cut the deal."

"But Elvis said he saw two guys talking with him in the store."

"That was Kenny Joseph, our runner. I like to think if I'd been there, this would have never happened, but"—he shakes his head—"I don't know. This is a hell of a bike." He reaches for a folded paper tucked into the back of his biking shorts, handing it to Bo. "Bill of sale," he says. "Your dad wanted it legit. Take it."

Bo holds up his hands, palms out. "Tell you what. You let me ride this thing today, I'd feel right if you kept it. Hell, biking is my weak leg. You're the real thing. It wouldn't be right for the likes of me to own a bike like this."

Lonnie smiles. "That's fair," he says, gripping Bo's bicycle by the handlebars, examining it quickly. "This ain't bad," he says. "I can kick your butt on this."

"Go for it," Bo says. "I'm coming after Joseph and Wyrack. One question."

"Yeah?"

"You said *first* your dad asked you whether you wanted to get into this war. What was second?"

"My dad and I get along good," Lonnie says. "He's always let me find my own way. He asked how I'd feel if the tables were turned—if some stranger stepped between the two of us. Then he said if I ever want to see how something works, look at it broken." He shrugs and turns to walk away.

Bo watches Lonnie walk his bike across the lot. *Look at it broken.*

Lonnie waves, looking back over his shoulder. "The next loud noise you hear will be Wyrack grunting his drawers when I tell him. By the way, nice hat. What's a Stotan?"

"You're about to find out," Bo yells back.

Hudgie looks as out of place in the Yukon Jack's River Resort parking lot as he does anywhere else in the world, resplendent in a pair of three-sizes-too-large Boy Scout hiking shorts and calf-high riding boots with gray-and-red striped wool socks peeking over the top and a T-shirt sporting a likeness of Elvis Presley with rhinestones for eyes and the caption THE KING. He carries what, from Bo's distant vantage point, looks to be automatic sealant for inner tubes in an aerosol can. Bo is aware that Hudge likes to keep symbolic things around him, whether he's participating in a particular event or not.

At the opposite end of the lot from Hudge, Elvis—in jeans and an identical Elvis Presley T-shirt—mills around the equipment area where individual contestants bag their gear to ready it to be transported to the transition areas and relay teams make final arrangements to make the exchange. Bo swings his leg over the Ultra-Lite and pedals it toward the highway to get a feel for the ride. He sees his mother's car drive into the parking lot as he coasts toward the two-lane. Forty-five minutes until start time.

On the open road, he runs quickly through the gears, noting the smooth precision and responsiveness, and a sharp mix of sadness and anger fill his chest as he ponders the idea of his father giving someone something this wonderful in order to beat him.

It ain't gonna happen, Dad. It ain't gonna happen.

Yukon Jack is in his splendor. Decked out in the formal uniform of the Royal Canadian Mounted Police, he fires his starter's pistol at the deep blue Columbia Basin sky to call the contestants to the starting line. He gazes out over the field of fewer than two hundred individual contestants and twenty-three relay teams. "Welcome to Yukon Jack's!" he booms. "I see by the scarcity of human bein's present that we've once again weeded out the weak sisters by puttin' the swimmin' last and doublin' the distance. Good, 'cause we got beer-guzzlin' an' snake-throwin' and cow-pie-eatin' contests for those folks. What I see here in front of me is the cream of the crop, I reckon. Now I hope you all got your support teams in place to pick up your bikes an' your runnin' gear at the proper transition areas. Remember, this race don't double back, so you're gonna finish a ways on down the river."

A loud skirmish breaks out just behind the group of contestants, and Bo whirls to the shrill resonance of Hudgie's voice. "Let me go! Let me go, you bastard! I'll kill you! Let me go!"

Bo works his way quickly to a small rise that allows him to see Wyrack gripping Hudgie's arm as the aerosol can Bo thought was tire-repair equipment clangs to the pavement. Elvis is sprinting across the parking lot, booming, "Let him go! Let him go!"

"Son of a bitch is spray painting my tank suit!" Wyrack yells back. "And Kenny's runnin' stuff!" He shakes Hudgie like a stern father. "What the hell is the matter with you, buddy?"

Elvis reaches them, and Bo expects big trouble. Ian Wyrack is a big, strong athlete, but that is no match for Elvis's history. But Elvis simply says, "It's okay, man. He's my brother. He's not right." He points to his head. "Does crazy shit like this all the time. I'm sorry, man, really sorry. I'll pay for the shirt."

Some of Wyrack's steam subsides. "Forget it. Just keep the creep away from me."

"No sweat, man," Elvis says. He grabs Hudgie roughly by the arm. "C'mon, little brother. I told you to stay out of trouble. I told you . . ." and they walk out of range. Bo sees Hudgie dance a quick little twist and shout, and Elvis's hand patting his back.

"Okay, folks," Yukon Jack says. "Just a little distraction, part of the festivities. It's all over. No harm done, 'cept you'll know exactly where that team is at any point in the race. That's a fine bright orange. Everything okay back there now, boys?"

Wyrack waves and shakes his head in disgust.

Yukon Jack continues with the race instructions. "Now you support-team folks remember, you cain't help your man or woman in the transition areas in any way that involves physically touching 'em. I mean, you can hand 'em a banana or a quick shot of whiskey, but don't be rubbin' down their shoulders or havin' sex or anything.

"You pansies—by that I mean all you relay team members— start with the individuals, and remember, you got to make physical contact with your teammate on the relay. Okay, you all know the rules, let's get out there and kill yourselves. An' have a real nice day."

Bo pulls his bicycle helmet—a triathlon requirement—tight over his STOTAN hat and moves into an advantageous position for the starting gun. Seconds ago he watched Wyrack, scowling, jump into his Storm and head off to drop Kenny Joseph at the runners' transition area before continuing on to his own, down the river several miles. He flashed his middle finger to Lonnie Gerback on his way out of the lot, and Gerback waved and yelled at Wyrack to swim fast. Bo smiled and adjusted his helmet, then felt a hand on his arm. "You got a nice butt in those cycling pants," Shelly said, and slapped it. "Go get 'em, Ironman."

Space is tight at the sound of the gun, with cyclists sprinting toward the narrow parking lot exit. Bo turns the corner onto the two-lane with the leaders and is forced wide to the other side of the road, where he finds himself staring at his father's face through the window of his gold Lexus, parked on the shoulder. Riding shotgun is Keith Redmond. Bo looks away and pours it on.

He is a quarter mile into the race when he remembers to reach behind him and punch play on the Walkman. "I knew you be forgettin' in the heat of the moment of the bang." Shuja's voice is like a Lionel Richie melody in the earphones. "But don't worry 'cause I made time allowances for jus' that. I been researchin' this cycling game a bit, an' soon as you get up to speed, kick this sweet thing into whatever gear gives you eighty rev-o-lu-shuns per minute, uphill, downhill, however the land may go.

"Now this may cause you pain, but these nex' three tunes give you the perfect beat. They rap, man, so they elegance may be lost on you, but *get . . . the . . . beat.*" The music plays about fifteen seconds before Shuja's voice again cuts in. "An' don' be reachin' for the forward button, my man. This whole piece of art be *timed.*"

The tape blasts out music Bo has never heard before, but he falls into cadence with the powerful bass and clicks into the corresponding gear on the bike. The front-runners have gone out hard, and the bike feels powerfully smooth beneath him as he settles in with the leaders of the second grouping. Ahead, he glimpses a fluorescent orange stripe the length of Gerback's back as he pulls slowly but steadily ahead. Lonnie must have allowed Hudge to spray one on him, too. "Keep you eye on the orange, Ironman," Shuja's voice croons to him over the music. "Eye on the orange."

Though the bike leg of the race is certainly Bo's weakest, he pushes to finish among the top quarter of competitors. Yukon Jack was right: The long swim at the end of this race weeds out weekend triathletes. This group will be composed of better-than-decent swimmers, and he needs to stay as far toward the front of the pack as possible.

The third song in Shuja's set is a repeat of the first. "Sorry, Ironman," he says at its conclusion. "Only fin' two songs with the perfect beat. Turnin' it over now. Rap with you later."

The next two songs are driving pieces by Waylon Jennings and Emmylou Harris, followed by Nak's easy Texas drawl. "When they told me to put somethin' on this here tape I thought might speed you along," he says, "I figured if you're like most kids I know, a good shot of this hard-core country music will make you hurry so you can get the damn earphones off." A short pause is followed by "An' seriously, Beauregard, we're all in your head here, but this race belongs to you. Now you hustle up an' make yourself proud."

Nak's voice is followed by more country tunes as Bo pedals into a long, steep climb and the river falls away to the right. The elite group of riders is out of sight about a half mile ahead around a hairpin turn now, led by Lonnie Gerback, and Bo is temporarily unable to keep his eye on the orange.

$\mathbf{B}$o pedals into the riverside park area serving as the transition area between the bike and the run to the soft strains of the *Moonlight* Sonata. He has held a position toward the middle of the second pack, far from sight of the leaders but in the top thirty percent overall, a little behind his projected status. His wind is good, and he feels generally strong but for the burning in his thighs from the uphill finish.

"What the hell?" the *Moonlight* Sonata is not exactly pump-up music.

Hudgie voices over, struggling for a soft, sleepytime tone. "Hey there, Mr. Ironman guy, relax." Bo hears Elvis in the background, coaching. "Follow up your nice leisurely ride with a little jog." There is a brief pause while Hudge takes instruction, then, "Your girlfriend, that muscle lady, said if you lose to those dumb college kids, she's mine. So take your time, Mr. Ironman. Stretch out." Pause. "Pull off to the side of the road and take a little snooze. You can live the rest of your life in cebalcy—what? What'd you say? Cebilacy?—cebilacy." In the background, Elvis says, "*Celibacy*, you idiot. Celibacy." Hudgie says "Cebilcy" and pauses. Then, "No sex, sucker."

Elvis from the background: "Good."

Bo laughs as he racks the bicycle, flipping off his helmet and readjusting the earphones. Shelly and Shuja stand in the support team area, she with a banana, he with a stopwatch. Shelly hands him the banana, peeled. "Looking good, big boy."

"Three minutes, fifty-eight seconds," Shuja hollers, giving Bo the length of Kenny Joseph's lead. Pick up a half minute per mile, Bo thinks, and I'll be close enough for a shot at Wyrack. It's possible. He's seen Kenny run, and though Kenny is easily a sub-seven-minute miler, Bo doubts he can hold it much under six and a half. Bo himself should be right at, or a little under, six minutes.

Depending on how long it takes to get his legs back. They are, at the moment, like rubber at the knees—a phenomenon with which most triathletes are familiar—and a crucial part of the race for Bo is leg recovery speed.

Running out of the transition area he holds a short stride and tries to relax, mentally alerting his legs that their task has been altered. He'll lose valuable time in the first mile that must be made up later. Because he didn't bike, Kenny Joseph did not go through this.

Bo turns the first wide corner of the run, about a quarter of a mile out of the transition area, as the *Moonlight* Sonata draws to its quiet close and Hudgie says, "Only foolin', Mr. Ironman, the muscle lady didn't really say that. Wish she did, though."

The host of Yukon Jack's radio extravaganza returns. "You best be runnin' by now, Beauregard. If you ain't, you damn well better be peddlin' like Redmond got your honey tied to the tracks, 'cause you got you some serious catchin' up to do." Pause. "But I'm bettin' you're runnin'. Now I'm gonna give you a little ol'-time white-bread music, like what Rock 'n' Roll like. Hate to do that to you, but I was badly outvoted. Hard for a African-American to win an election in these parts."

Bob Seger's "Old Time Rock and Roll" pounds into Bo's ears, and he hits a stride to fit that urgent beat, willing his biking muscles to give over to the run.

Seger hammers to a close, and Shuja is back. "Okay," he says. "Legs should be good by now. Got to get you back in this a little at a time. You down twenty points, you bring 'em back one hoop, then another. Don't start firin' three-pointers like a man in panic. Lock your eyes on some wobbly fish up there about a hunnerd yards." Pause. "Now start reelin' 'im in. Good an' solid, jus' reel 'im in. When you got 'im in the boat, they's plenty more fish where he from. Reel 'em in."

Bo focuses on a runner in a bright red shirt about a football field ahead of him, and steadily increases his cadence. *Here we go.*

He pulls alongside the red shirt to the tune of Bryan Adams's "Summer of '69" and searches the waters in the distance for another fish.

The ten-kilometer run winds along a wide, calm section of the river, through rugged and starkly beautiful country. Across the river craggy bluffs reach toward a crystal blue sky. Identical bluffs climb straight up from the two-lane highway, and the fifty-nine-degree temperature allows the contestants to kill themselves in near-perfect conditions.

Bo is renewed as he passes runner after runner whose strong leg was the cycling. Heading into the final three kilometers, he watches less conditioned athletes show early signs of fading, all the time searching for Hudgie's fluorescent orange stripe down the back of Kenny Joseph's running gear to tell him he's got a clear shot at Ian Wyrack once he hits the water. A glance at his Ironman wristwatch tells him his per-mile average is right at six minutes, and he ever-so-slightly increases the pace, set on forcing it a few seconds under. He's reeling them in one by one now, feeling that powerful second wind he's been building for all winter long.

A sexy whisper drifts into his ear: "If you win this, we'll have sex." Shelly. Bo knows she's kidding, but the thought throws fire into him. It will be fun watching her back down. He makes a note to tell Redmond he was wrong about having to give up girlfriends prior to or during peak athletic contests. Old myths die hard.

"Bo Brewster is a quitter." The familiar, grating voice of Keith Redmond, over the Beach Boys singing "Be True to Your School." "When given the opportunity to perform for his school, a chance to do his best for the glory of the Blackhawks and himself, to really show what he was made of, he quit. Pure and simple, he quit."

"There you go, Beauregard," Shuja says. "Could have put my black ass in a sling for at least eternity gettin' that one for you. But call me Shaft; Coach Death don't even know I be wired when he said it. Don't stop to thank me, just run you ass off."

Spectators line the roadway now, cheering, telling Bo he is within a half-mile of the run-swim transition area. He catches a quick glimpse of Kenny Joseph's bright orange stripe seconds before Kenny disappears around the final sharp curve, and adrenaline runs through him like a river. Two down and one to go, and he's within striking range.

And then somebody pulls his plug. His feet turn to anvils, and air squirts in and out of his lungs like molasses. His cadence drops as if someone has released his throttle and jammed his brakes to the floorboard. Terrible hunger gnaws. Within fifteen seconds of his adrenaline high, Bo Brewster is being fitted for a lead suit.

Can't panic. He knows these sensations from other overextended runs. *Too far too fast.* Did he misread his initial energy? Pay too much attention to the tape and not enough to his body? Try to do it all too early? *It passes. It gets over. Hold on.* As if by summons, Lion is in his headset. "You got nothin' to prove to anybody but yourself, big man. Stotanism is a state of being, and you're there. All you have to do now is celebrate it. I've watched you in the water for the better part of a year now, and I have *never* seen you back off. Never. Go down into the part that drives you, Bo, into the engine of your soul. Enjoy this. You own it."

You own it. You own it. This gets over. Shit.

Lion is followed by Elvis. "Hey, Ironman. Jury's still out on you, man, but you got a chance to strike a blow for every ragin' beat-up son of a bitch in our group, and maybe in the world. That's a chance not many guys get. Don't screw it up."

Bo pictures his friends, his fellow Stotans, the members of Nak's Pack running with him. The truth is, their lives will go on—pretty much unchanged—whether he wins or not. He could give in to this evil vacuum sucking his life out, and time will march on. But then there's Hudge. What must it mean to

173

Hudge to participate in this? To belong, to have a hand in someone striking a blow for *him*? Each time his voice comes over the headset, there is a childlike, barely contained giddiness. How many times in Hudge's life will he have a chance to walk the edge of something this powerful? The thoughts are complete, but they flash into Bo's brain in split seconds.

Tell somebody who cares. I've still got two miles in the river. Bo rounds the final curve breathing deep, deep breaths, sucking oxygen into his bowels. *I've never seen you back down. Not once.* Three hundred yards ahead, Shelly and Shuja stand waiting, bananas and Gatorade at the ready, waving him in. Beyond them a blur of contestants strip to their swimming suits, dashing into the cold river. He slows, relaxing his legs for the switch and the possibility of leg cramps. He overloaded with potassium and calcium and salt this morning, but the nature of the flutter kick—toes down, feet extended—is a written prescription for knots in the calves. He will swim with only his arms for the first four hundred yards or so, then add legs as his body accommodates the conversion. *If I can just get past this wall!*

His overheated body and brain are thrilled at the sight of contestants hitting the cold water, and the possibility of new life presents itself. *God, don't let me be drained. Let it pass. Let it pass.*

And suddenly it's four-thirty in the morning. Familiar theme music bounces into his head, followed by "Bo Brewster, this is Larry King. I read your manuscript, but I can't make a decision until I see the final chapter. You've got some girlfriend there; says you didn't even know she read it. Don't be mad at her for sending it; it's good. I want you to know I passed up the parts you said were confidential. I, of all people, respect privacy. At any rate, you hurry up and kick this Wyrack guy's butt, and we'll book a program about Stotans and Gladiators, or maybe fathers and sons. They tell me you should be looking at the river as you hear this, so I'll shut up, and you get on your way."

Larry King theme music fades, and Bo Brewster, laughing

like a maniac, grabs a banana and his goggles from Shelly, takes a long swig of Shuja's Gatorade, pulls the plug on the earphones as he drops the tune belt to the dirt, sails the Stotan hat toward his father—standing near the shore beside Keith Redmond—and charges into the Columbia River in pursuit of Ian Wyrack, who's about to fall five hundred green ones into debt.

EPILOGUE

Dear Larry,

Hey, Lar, you saved my life. I came stumbling into the run-swim transition area running on empty, and your voice resurrected me. I did as you bid, Lar. I kicked that Wyrack guy's butt, finished well above the middle of the pack. I caught a glimpse of Hudge's fluorescent orange stripe down the back of his suit about a half mile from the finish and I played "Larry King Live" theme music in my head and just swam him down.

I would have written sooner, Lar, but the final chapter didn't end with the race, and until today I couldn't have wrapped it up in any way that would have made sense. Now I can.

I haven't decided where I'll go to school next year, or even if I'll go to school. The night after Yukon Jack's, Shelly and I drove back up the river to the place I camped the night before, and we laid our sleeping bags together and stared at the stars and had our dreams. She said she knows people laugh at her idea of being an American Gladiator sometimes, but she doesn't care; it's going to happen. "You can't know what it's like to be completely disregarded, Bo," she said. "Maybe some of it has to do with being female in a culture where women's voices don't have volume, but when you lost football, it was a blessing. When Redmond took basketball from me, he stole my soul. I was young then, I was small. But I'm big now, and I can get it back."

I love her, Lar, I really do. Enough to have enrolled in a high-impact dance aerobics class with her that is going to test the Ironman in me, as well as my ability to keep my eyes on the instructor and off the thong leotards well

176

within reach in front of me, but out of reach if you know what I mean.

Dad was nowhere to be found when I rose out of the water like King Neptune at the finish of Yukon Jack's, so I didn't get a chance to say all the things I wanted to say that I'd have to take back later. But Mom and Jordan were there—along with the rest of the Angry Management Brigade—and Mom just ran and threw her arms around me and soaked her blouse against my dripping body. Jordan said he liked riding down with Mr. S, because he doesn't like girls either. I think I need to clear that up. At first I thought Dad was being a poor loser, but later I thought maybe he split because he saw me on the Ultra-Lite and didn't want to discuss where it came from. From race day until graduation we avoided the topic like *E. coli.*

But then he asked what I wanted for a graduation present, and I told him I wanted him to go into counseling with me. I didn't really want that, but Mr. S told me I did and I believed him. When I asked, Dad said no way, but he walked up to me in the high school gym the night of the ceremony and handed me an appointment card.

We went to a guy named Dr. Jorgensen in Spokane—a guy Mr. Nak recommended—and he was something else. Sometimes we went together and sometimes we went separately, but when we entered his room, there was no right and wrong, no good guys or bad guys, no judgment. We simply told our stories. Turns out Dad fought his father the way I fight him, and I think I got a true glimpse of my dad as a boy, and I'm afraid we're a lot alike.

That scares me, Lar, because it means I could end up like him, and I don't want that; I believe my father leads a desperate life. In our last session he told a story of his dad punishing him for leaving a corral gate open, allowing some cattle to roam free. Their bull was hit by a semi out on the interstate, and it cost Grampa several thousand dollars. He made Dad brace his back against the kitchen wall in a sitting position—with no chair under him—for more than a half hour. Sweat poured off Dad's forehead as he recounted his story, and his voice choked nearly into silence. He screamed at Grampa that he hated him and would never close another gate on the whole goddamn ranch, and Grampa whipped his trembling legs with a willow switch. Dad didn't give in, though; he never sat down.

Dr. Jorgensen turned to me and asked if I ever felt about my dad the way Dad had just described his feelings about Grampa, and I started to say yes, but one look into his face made me cut it off. He saw my response in my eyes, though, and he stood, shook Dr. Jorgensen's hand, and said he wouldn't be coming back. He said, "This is too hard." I haven't seen him since then, and I don't know how I feel about that.

Mr. Nak is leaving. He's going back to Texas. In what has to be one of the most significant nights of my life, Mr. Nak pulled this all together for me.

A week or so after graduation he asked all the members of the anger management group to come to another evening meeting. I recorded everything said that night, Lar, because Mr. Nak's words have come to mean a lot to me, and I wanted to remember everything right.

Mr. S was with him when he walked into the room wearing his customary denim shirt and Levis, boots clicking on the hardwood floor, in that easy manner I've come to feel so safe with, and he asked everyone—including Mr. S—to sit in the same circle we've been in all along, and he sat up on his desk, like always, and said, "I'm gonna be movin' on, so I thought I'd get ever one together an' say my piece.

"I been doin' this anger management thing for years, an' it's probably the most important thing I do in the world of education. Hell, anybody can teach you how to fix a busted engine or build a damn shoebox. This here last anger management group was different than all the rest, an' I need to say that. I feel honored to have watched some of your work.

"I know your stories a lot better than you know mine, an' I want you to know, no matter where I go, those stories are safe with me. But I'm gonna even things up a little this evenin' an' tell you mine." Then he told us a story that I can't detail right now, Lar, because I just don't want to feel as bad as I'd have to to tell it.

It boils down to Mr. Nak driving drunk one night when he was a young man, and he killed his kids.

When he finished his story, he said, "I don't tell y'all that for sympathy, because ain't no sympathy in the world gonna make it one bit different for me. I tell it because there seems to be a tendency for my groups to walk away thinkin' I got a bunch of wisdom, an' I dispense it like some kind of cowboy god. Well, I ain't no god, not even a little bit, an' I don't want nobody thinkin' that, because it cheapens what I have to offer."

He said, "I always kinda wanted to be a preacher, but I ain't never had no particular religion to preach, an' that leaves me at a disadvantage in that regard. But I got something to preach about anyway, an' since I tricked y'all into comin' tonight, I'm gonna let fly." He paused a minute and looked around the group. "This group has taught me more about the nature of mercy than I've learned since the night I sat in a dark room upstairs in my house and decided not to end my own life like I done my children's. I think not many people understand the nature of mercy, because it gets misnamed a lot—hooked up with organized religions when there ain't no call for that—but I see it as the only medicine available for what ails us, so I need to prescribe it. It is the only medicine for our anger, it is the only medicine for our hurt, it is the only medicine for our desperation."

Mr. Nak rose, put a finger in the air, and said, "The nature of mercy allows for all things. It excuses nothing, but it allows for all things. It allows for a young man full of drink to push his luck and explode his universe, it allows for a son to stand in disobedience before his father, an' it allows for a man's meanness in trying to break that son's spirit in the name of fatherhood.

"It allows an anger management guru the mistake of tryin' to get some unsuspectin' kid to let a skunk into his house, an' it allows the insensitivity of an educator to steal a young girl's athletic dreams. It allows a man to molest his daughter an' desert his family." He looked directly at Mr. S. "An' it allows for a boy to jump out of the boat." He nodded. "It does, Lion, man."

Shelly shook her head. "Mr. Nak, what about Hudgie's burns? How can anything allow for that?"

Mr. Nak smiled. He said, "It allows for all things, Shelly. Remember I said it don't excuse any of 'em."

I don't think everyone understood all Mr. Nak was saying, Lar. I know some of it was unclear to me, but the group was almost reverently silent. Mr. Nak sat back on his desk and said, "Ya know, I've heard folks say 'Life's not fair' in this group a lot. I've even said it myself when the occasion seemed to call for it. But that ain't correct. Life is exactly fair. *People* ain't fair, but life sure as hell is. Most of us just ain't willin' to accept it. Life has Ironmen an' Stotans an' American Gladiators, an' Charles Mansons an' Jeffrey Dahmers. Life has ever kind of holy man an' devil. If you're ever gonna beat all the anger an' hurt inside you, you're gonna have to learn to offset the awful with the magnificent. But that requires allowin' for both to have their place in the world. An' whether you allow it or not, it's there. The truth don't need you to believe it for it to be true.

"I said earlier I'm hittin' the trail. Let me tell you why. I'm goin' back to Texas. They got a senior rodeo circuit down there I can join up with. I'm goin' because of what I saw at Yukon Jack's. I been payin' less attention to the physical world than I should, gettin' outta contact. When I saw young Brewster here workin' his way through that hellish event, it got me to rememberin' what it was like to be on a bareback bronc, how it felt to know exactly where that thunderous devil was goin' next, just from the tension in his muscle against my knee. I been payin' attention to other folks' lives—an' learnin' some while I was at it—but now it's time to start payin' attention to my own agin. I wanna thank you folks for teachin' me that. I owe ya, an' I'll stay on a bronc one second longer in each of your names."

Then he got up and walked out of the room, Lar. I've never seen him again.

So there's your last chapter. Mercy allows for all things. Today I rode my bicycle over the back road to Spokane and out the Centennial Trail toward Idaho, and on the way back I passed the building where Dr. Jorgensen has his office. I saw my dad's Lexus parked outside.

I don't know what will come of that—hell, Dad might have been there arguing about the bill—and I don't have any expectations. But no matter what happens, I'll survive, and I won't lead a desperate life, because the eight months I spent with that posse of ragamuffin Stotans led by an undersized Japanese cowboy gave me the power to let the world be every bit as goddamn crazy as it is.

Be well, Larry King,

Beauregard Brewster